"You can't call time in the middle of a pitch!" the ump barked from the dirt.

Tugboat didn't say a word. As the hitter took off for first, he just pointed to center field. We whipped our heads around to see what was bothering him. All except Stump Plumwhiff, our shortstop, that is. As I turned, I saw Stump charge the slow roller coming his way and rush a throw to our first baseman, Gilly Wishes.

Then I looked to the outfield to see what had caused Tugboat to act so strangely.

What I witnessed made my knees quake.

A huge, shimmering cloud filled the sky. Shaped sort of like an ice-cream cone lying on its side, it stretched all the way to the horizon. Whatever it was, it was moving.

Fast.

Straight toward us.

KEVIN MARKEY

HARPER

An Imprint of HarperCollins*Publishers*

The Super Sluggers: Wing Ding

www.harpercollinschildrens.com

Library of Congress Cataloging-in-Publication Data
Markey, Kevin.

Wing ding / Kevin Markey. — 1st ed.

p.   cm. — (The super sluggers)

Summary: When star shortstop for the Rambletown Rounders, Stump Plumwhiff, comes down with
a bad case of the "yips," his teammates try to help him
regain his self-confidence before the All-Star game.

ISBN 978-0-06-115227-6

[1. Baseball—Fiction.   2. Self-confidence—
Fiction.] I. Title.
PZ7.M3394546Wi 2011   2010015901
[Fic]—dc22   CIP
                                                       AC

Typography by Larissa Lawrynenko
12 13 14 15 16   CG/BR   10 9 8 7 6 5 4 3 2 1
❖
First paperback edition, 2012

For Sarah and Nat,
with love

★ CHAPTER 1 ★

Tugboat Tooley spotted it first.

Tugboat plays catcher for the Ramble-town Rounders baseball team, reigning champs of the ten-to-twelve division.

I play third base.

My name is the Great Walloper, Walloper for short. At least that's what everybody calls me, because I like to wallop the tar out of the ball. My real name, the one my parents gave me, is Banjo. Banjo H. Bishbash, to be precise. The *H* stands for Hit. People ask me about my name all the time. "So unusual," they say.

It gets tiring.

For the record, Hit was my mom's last name before she married my dad. Banjo is my grandfather's name and my dad's, too. Like the musical instrument. For real.

You can see why I prefer Walloper.

At the moment I wasn't worried about any of that. I was more concerned with keeping the St. Joe Jungle Cats from tying the score.

It was the top of the third inning, no outs, a fair breeze blowing straight in from center. Our pitcher, Slingshot Slocum, stood on the mound protecting a slim 2–1 lead. A St. Joe runner bounced on his toes at second base. From the way he kept glancing in my direction, I knew he was thinking about stealing third.

Crouched behind home plate, Tugboat surveyed the diamond. Nothing gets past Tugboat. Not balls, not base runners, not even the hot-dog man out in the bleachers making change for a five spot. Tugboat's our field general and we rely on him.

A real general would have been nice. He would've had an army at his command. As we were about to learn, we could've used an army. Maybe the air force, too. Send in the marines just to be safe.

Tugboat flashed a sign. One finger. That meant fastball. A fastball is not a good pitch to steal on. It gets to the plate too quickly. If Slingshot blazed the ball home and Tugboat made a good peg to me, we'd have a good shot at cutting down the runner. All I had to do was make a clean catch and apply the tag.

I shot a look toward second. I wondered if the runner could see Tugboat's signals as clearly as I could. I hoped not.

At the plate, the St. Joe hitter, batting lefty, dug into the box. He zeroed in on Slingshot like a laser beam. The umpire hunkered down behind Tugboat, one hand resting lightly on the catcher's right shoulder for balance. The ump, too, was completely focused on Slingshot.

Slingshot kicked and fired a fastball. The St. Joe batter started his swing.

That's when Tugboat sprang from behind the plate.

"Time out!" he called, flinging away his mask.

3

He bounced up so quickly, I thought a bee had stung him.

Tugboat's sudden leap knocked the ump backward, toppling him onto his backside behind home plate. I don't know what the ump thought. Probably how much he was going to enjoy tossing Tugboat out of the game. While all this was happening, the batter lunged at the pitch and sent the ball dribbling toward short.

"You can't call time in the middle of a pitch!" the ump barked from the dirt.

Tugboat didn't say a word. As the hitter took off for first, he just pointed to center field. We whipped our heads around to see what was bothering him. All except Stump Plumwhiff, our shortstop, that is. As I turned, I saw Stump charge the slow roller coming his way and rush a throw to our first baseman, Gilly Wishes.

Then I looked to the outfield to see what had caused Tugboat to act so strangely.

What I witnessed made my knees quake.

A huge, shimmering cloud filled the sky.

Shaped sort of like an ice-cream cone lying on its side, it stretched all the way to the horizon. Whatever it was, it was moving.

Fast.

Straight toward us.

The leading edge, where the cone came to a point, dived straight over the high wooden outfield fence. A second later a terrible noise filled my ears. The sound grew louder and louder as the spiraling black thing swirled closer and closer. It buzzed like a million vacuum cleaners sucking up everything in their path.

"What in the world is that?" I shouted.

"It's an error," Stump said dejectedly as his throw sailed over Gilly's head and into the grandstand.

Stump and I always talk out on the diamond. Usually we stick to baseball chatter. "Two, four, six, eight, our pitcher's looking great!" Stuff like that. "Batter, batter, what's the matter? Swing, batter!"

"Forget the throw," I said, pointing toward

5

the outfield. "What is that thing?"

Stump looked up and finally caught his first glimpse of the buzzing cone. His eyes were only a little bigger than stop signs as he said, "Walloper, I do believe it's a tornado!"

"I never saw a tornado that moved side-ways," I shouted back over the rising din.

In fact I had never seen a tornado at all except in movies. This didn't look like any Hollywood twister.

We call Stump "Stump" because he has an answer for everything. You can never stump him. If he doesn't know the answer, he makes one up. If Stump said this thing was a tornado, I was prepared to believe him.

"Run for your lives!" I shouted.

My teammates were way ahead of me.

Literally.

Most of them were already halfway to our low concrete dugout on the third-base side of the diamond. The St. Joe base runners chugged past us going the other way. They didn't bother to stay inside the base paths. It looked more like a footrace than a baseball game.

Just then a remote-control helicopter fell out of the sky. It landed with a whine, smack in the middle of the diamond.

Another one plunged to the ground behind it. Then another and another.

An armor-plated green one swooped down and knocked Stump's cap off his head as he scrambled for cover. One thing you should know about Stump: he practically never takes off his cap. He wears it summer and winter, day and night. He probably wears it in the shower. The sight of his stand-up red hair was shocking.

But not nearly as shocking as what was dropping onto the field.

It wasn't helicopters at all. It was grass-hoppers. Millions and millions of huge grasshoppers.

My first reaction was relief. That massive black cloud wasn't a tornado after all. My second was a severe case of the heebie-jeebies:

bugs covered every inch of the field. More poured over the fence every second. In the stands, screaming fans climbed all over each other to reach the exits.

The umpire waved his hands in the air.

"I'm calling the game," he said. "It's canceled due to grasshoppers."

Then he kicked up his heels and joined the mass exodus from Rambletown Field. Within a few minutes, the ballpark was completely deserted. Deserted by fans, that is. The insect population had never been higher.

From the safety of the dugout, my teammates and I watched the cloud of bugs settle on the field. It was like having a front-row ticket to one of those nature programs on the Animal Channel on TV: "When Grasshoppers Attack!"

Except that it was real.

And it was live.

And instead of in some far-off savanna in Africa or wherever, it was happening right here in Rambletown.

★ CHAPTER 2 ★

Mr. Bones scrambled out from under the long aluminum bench and dashed around the dugout like he wanted to be on a TV show of his own. "Dancing with the Dogs" I would've called it.

Mr. Bones is my dog. He's a short-legged, long-nosed, yellow-haired fur ball that strangers often mistake for a bandicoot. He loves to be petted and he loves to lick faces. Judging by the way he snapped at the insects flitting through the air, he does not love grasshoppers.

"Easy, boy," I said.

I patted the bench. Wagging his tail like a flyswatter, Mr. Bones jumped up next to me.

A real flyswatter would have been nice. We

could have used it against the bugs.

On my other side, Stump slouched deject-edly, still stewing over his bad throw. My buddy had recovered his hat but not his composure.

"I can't believe I muffed that play," he grum-bled. His face was as red as the hair hidden beneath his lid. "Hanley Ramirez would have made that play. Troy Tulowitzki would have nailed it."

Stump kept close tabs on Major League shortstops. He knew all the stats of everyone who'd ever played the position. Kind of fright-ening, really, the way he could rattle off their numbers.

"Forget it, will you? We have worse things to worry about right now," Slingshot said.

"What's worse than a throwing error on a shortstop?" Stump asked. "E6 on a routine grounder! I airmailed the ball right into the stands!"

Every defensive position in baseball has a number. Six is the number for shortstop. *E* stands for error.

"*Melanoplus* is worse," said Slingshot.

"Say what?" asked Ocho James, our powerful right fielder. His eyes did not waver from the diamond. There were more bugs out there than grains of sand on a beach. Real sand would have been nice. As far as I know, there's no such thing as a sandhopper.

"*Melanoplus sanguinipes*," said Slingshot, shouting to make himself heard over the buzz of mashing insects. "The fabled migratory grasshopper. Otherwise known as a locust."

Slingshot knows a lot of scientific stuff. He knows a lot of everything, as a matter of fact, but science is his favorite subject. He plucked a stray insect off his uniform sleeve and cupped it in his hands.

The ugly invader measured about one inch long. It had two short antennae, plastic-looking wings that folded along its back, and a pair of spring-loaded legs. But what really grabbed your attention was the wedge-shaped head. With its bulging black alien eyes and powerful jaw, the noggin could have come straight out of a science-fiction movie. The jaw looked like it could do some damage.

"Nasty-looking critter," said Kid Rabbit Winkle, our all-around infielder and top pinch hitter.

"In the summer," said Slingshot, "they sometimes migrate in huge swarms."

"Why?" Gabby asked, flipping open her notebook.

Gabby Hedron is my friend and classmate at Rambletown Elementary. She also covers sports for the *Rambletown Bulletin*, the local newspaper, which is why she happened to be in the dugout with the team.

"Usually to find food."

"How do they know where to look for it?" asked Ellis "the Glove" Rodriguez, the team's crackerjack second baseman.

"I believe they follow wind currents," Slingshot yelled. The bugs were truly deafening. "They go where it carries them and take what they can get."

Gabby, nodding, scribbled some notes. "The wind has been blowing from the west for a couple days," she said.

"You make them sound all carefree and whatnot, like pirates or something," chimed in Tugboat. "Yo-ho-ho, a grasshopper's life for me."

"Do they bite?" Billy asked nervously.

Billy Wishes is the kid brother of our first baseman, Gilly. Too young to actually play for the Rounders, he is our batboy. We love having him around. For one thing, he's always cheerful. For another, he's luckier than a six-footed rabbit. He's always finding cool stuff and winning prizes and junk like that. His good fortune has a way of rubbing off on the team. So far, though, the grasshoppers seemed immune to his charm. They continued to dive-bomb the field.

"Only wheat and grass and any other sweet, green thing they come across on their travels," Slingshot said. He opened his hand and flicked the insect toward the on-deck circle. Or where the circle would have been if it hadn't been buried beneath a carpet of chomping hoppers. "A single swarm can contain ten billion insects."

Gasser Phipps tilted his head to one side and tapped it with the heel of his hand as if he were clearing water from his ear after a swim. "Did you say ten *billion*?" our fleet outfielder gasped.

"That's what I heard, too," said Orlando "Velcro" Ramirez, the newest member of our team. He shares time in center with Gasser.

Velcro had joined the Rounders back in the freakishly cold spring, after Gasser broke his leg in a snowboarding accident. While Gasser mended, Velcro took over in center. His nickname gives a pretty good idea of how balls stick in his glove. His only problem was the green wooden fence that encircled Rambletown Field.

Throughout the snowy early season, the Rounders had been forced to practice on a frozen field. The wintry conditions gave Velcro fits. He came from Florida, where the only ice he ever saw came on sno-cones. Again and again, he lost his footing and slammed into the wall.

For a while it was touch and go as to which one would be left standing: the wall or Velcro. But that's a different story. Suffice it to say, Velcro survived. Once the field finally thawed out— with a little help from a giant solar reflector we rigged up—he found his footing and stopped knocking himself loopy. Most of the time, anyway. Occasionally he still flung himself at the wall like a human cannonball in order to make a spectacular catch.

"I did say ten billion," Slingshot confirmed.

"No way!" exclaimed Gasser. "That's more than every single man, woman, and child on earth!"

"Way," said Slingshot. "Just be glad they're so little and we're so big. Blow them up to human size and we wouldn't stand a chance."

I snapped my attention back to the field. Was this what ten billion insects looked like? The number was too big to compute. All you could say with certainty was that there were a lot of them.

A whole lot.

And they were hungry.

And they were treating our field like an all-you-can-eat salad bar.

Those suckers already had widened the base paths by a foot and stripped a big patch of outfield down to bare dirt.

"How do you get rid of them?" I asked, shouting to make myself heard.

"You don't," said Slingshot.

"What are you saying?" My voice rose. "They're going to stick around forever? Impossible!"

Didn't those grasshoppers know the league All-Star Game was less than a week away? And that it was going to be played at Rambletown Field? For the first time ever?

Our league put on an All-Star Game in the middle of every season. The previous year's champions always got to host it. Nine times out of ten, this meant the game took place in Hog City, home of the mighty Haymakers. Our archrivals were the biggest, meanest, hairiest team in history. On top of being big and mean and hairy, they were good. Really, really good. Led by ace pitcher Flicker Pringle, the scariest fastballer in the league, they racked up championships like the rest of us collected baseball cards. Those guys had closets full of trophies. But last year we'd beaten them in an epic contest and won our first title.

We were the champs.

Which meant we got to put on the All-Star Game right here at our home park.

We'd been looking forward to it ever since opening day. Stump, Ducks Bunion, and I had been named to the team. We couldn't wait to play in front of a home crowd. Playing alongside us would be the best of the best, including a few Haymakers.

Having those guys as teammates instead of mortal enemies would be weird. Normally we tried to beat each other's brains out. But the All-Star Game is different. It's a celebration of baseball. You put aside your rivalries for a day and go out and just play ball. It's an honor . . . and a blast.

And now a bunch of rotten bugs had infested the field! If they stuck around, the game would get canceled. Just like this one had.

"Oh, they'll leave," Slingshot assured us.

"Now you're talking," I said with relief. "After they rest their wings for a bit, right? A few more minutes and they're out of here?"

Slingshot shook his head. "I can think of two things that would drive them away," he said. "One is a whole lot of wind. I mean a really freakish storm, the kind that rips roofs off of barns. That would do it."

"What's the other?" I asked.

"They run out of stuff to eat."

We all looked at our pitcher to see if he was kidding. He returned our gaze with a stony stare. He was serious. Dead serious.

And so were the insects. They were serious about eating.

★ CHAPTER 3 ★

The next morning Rambletown Field starred in the daily paper. Rather, what was left of it did. A big picture on the front page of the *Rambletown Bulletin* showed our ballpark buried to the bleachers in chomping insects.

Small print beneath the picture identified Gabby as the photographer. In the course of following our team over the years, she had written about droughts, blizzards, heat waves, and a giant ice mountain. Now she added gobbling grasshoppers to the list.

Never a dull moment in Rambletown.

Her story said:

LUNCHING LOCUSTS LAY WASTE TO
BALL FIELD

Traveling like a home run in reverse, a swarm of greedy grass-grubbers sailed over the outfield wall at Rambletown Field yesterday afternoon. The invasion disrupted a tight game between the Rounders and the visiting Jungle Cats of St. Joe. After driving fans from the stands and players from the diamond, the beastly bugs proceeded to chow down on the field. Local insect expert and star pitcher Slingshot Slocum estimates the scaly scalawags may number ten billion. It'll take a hurricane to blow them away. Or something stronger. In the meantime, this weekend's All-Star Game is in trouble.

I tossed aside the paper and spooned up some Pirate Crunch from my breakfast bowl. The cereal was the kind with frosted cannonballs, which crackled as I chewed them. The sound reminded me of all those grinding locust jaws. I pushed away the bowl in disgust.

Mr. Bones darted over and stood beside my chair, his tail wagging a mile a minute. It was his way of asking if I was finished eating and if he could have what was left.

"Knock yourself out, pal," I said. I got up from the table and dumped my soggy cereal into his bowl. His tail swept the air like a broom as he buried his nose in milk-soaked Pirate Crunch.

A real broom would have been nice. A huge one. We could have used it to sweep away the bugs.

I supposed things could have been worse. We could have been infested by rattlesnakes. On the other hand, snakes would make for a pretty good home-field advantage. Other teams would be jumpy as kangaroos if they had to visit a field crawling with diamondbacks. Kangaroos can't play baseball worth beans. If we could master our own fear of snakes, we'd win every game by a landslide.

"Good morning, champ!"

My mom breezed into the kitchen. She wore gardening clothes. Dad followed right behind her. He was dressed for the office: jacket, tie, dark trousers. His tie was red with tiny green fishing lures embroidered all over it. The lures looked like insects. Or what a fisherman thinks a fish thinks an insect looks like. To me Dad's tie just looked like a bad joke.

"Is that supposed to be funny?" I asked.

"What's funny about ties?" he said. "I'd rather wear a T-shirt, but this morning I'm meeting with a guy who happens to love trout fishing."

"I thought maybe you were commenting on the situation over at Rambletown Field."

"The situation?"

"Grasshoppers, honey," Mom reminded him as she poured herself a cup of coffee.

Dad could be forgetful.

"Oh, right! Wow! Maybe I should go with stripes instead. I don't want people to get any wrong ideas about my loyalties. What's the latest on that?"

I showed my parents the paper. Dad whistled at the picture.

"They sure do look hungry," he said. "Speaking of hungry, how about an omelet?"

One thing my dad loved was making omelets for breakfast, the bigger the better. If the *Guinness Book of World Records* had an omelet category, Dad would own it. Normally, I loved eating his moon-sized creations. But not this morning. Thinking about those locusts munching away on our beautiful field had completely killed my appetite.

"I already ate," I said as Mr. Bones slurped up the rest of my Pirate Crunch.

"Just as well," Mom said, sounding relieved.

She popped a bagel into the toaster, then flipped on the radio. The rich voice of Louie "the Lip" Leibenstraub flooded the kitchen.

The Lip said:

"And now for the WHOT 102.5 Storm Team AccuWeather forecast. Batten down the hatches, folks, because we're in for a blow over the next few days. A tropical low-pressure system is parked to the north. Expect wind,

wind, and more wind, building to squall-like
force by tomorrow afternoon. Should make
for perfect conditions at the annual Ramble-
town Kite Festival this Friday!"

My ears pricked up. The kite festival was awesome. Every year it drew thousands of people to Rambletown Park. In the past I'd loved watching the amazing show. It would be a blast to actually enter a kite this year.

Even better than kites was the promise of wind. Slingshot had said a good blow could drive away the grasshoppers.

The Lip continued.

"In honor of the weather, let's go deep into
the vault for a blustery classic. Here's a little
ditty by Bob Dylan, voted the number-one
all-time wind song by our listeners. For more
weather updates and more great music, keep
it tuned to WHOT 102.5, the coolest station on
the planet."

"Wait a minute," interrupted Dad. "Rewind." He turned down the volume. "You don't like my omelets?"

"They're top notch," Mom said with a smile. She retrieved her bagel from the toaster and smeared some butter on it. "What I could live without is the aftermath. Last time you made one, it looked like a tornado had touched down in the kitchen after passing through a farm stand. Diced veggies everywhere."

A real tornado would've been nice. It would've taken care of the grasshoppers.

"Ouch," Dad said.

"Joke," said Mom soothingly. "Your omelets are world class." She put her bagel on a plate and turned up the radio again. Out poured a harmonica riff, followed by jangly guitar music. Then a cat with a head cold started to sing. At least that's what it sounded like to me. The cat moaned about the wind and some friend of his and how his friend blew an answer in the wind.

I had no idea what he was talking about.

I just hoped the grasshoppers would blow away with it.

"I love this song," Mom said, grabbing Dad by the hand and dancing him across the floor.

Smiling again, omelets forgotten, he raised Mom's hand in his own to make an arch, and she twirled under it.

"Gross," I said. Next thing you knew, they'd be holding hands in public. Mr. Bones did not see how wrong this was. He scrambled over and started darting around their feet as if he were trying to herd shoes.

"Don't encourage them," I said.

Dad started singing along with the radio. His voice was even worse than the other guy's. He howled about the wind and the mysterious answer floating on it.

I still didn't know what the question was.

The only one I could think of was about the All-Star Game. What would happen to it with our field in shambles?

★ CHAPTER 4 ★

I got an answer a couple hours later. A possible answer. And a lousy one at that. I did not get it from the wind, which by midmorning, however, definitely had picked up. An occasional gust rattled the window of my bedroom, where I sat anxiously taping and retaping the handle of my favorite Louisville Slugger and wishing for a hurricane.

Be careful of what you wish for, is all I can say.

I was working to get the bat ready for our game against the Hog City Haymakers the next day. I wanted everything to be perfect. It would be our final tune-up before the All-Star Game.

If there was going to be an All-Star Game.

We were scheduled to play in Hog City. I hoped the swarm wouldn't be an issue over there. As far as I knew, those greedy grass grubbers had invaded only Rambletown.

The phone rang. I dropped my stick and darted into the hall.

"What's up?" I said, expecting to hear Stump or Slingshot at the other end of the line.

"What's up yourself, Walloper?" replied a deep voice. "I've got some good news for you."

"Uh, good morning, Skip Lou," I said with a cough, recognizing my coach's voice.

Skip Lou coached the Rambletown Rounders. During the school year, he taught music at Rambletown Elementary. The nameplate on his door said Mr. Clementine, but to members of the Rounders he would always be Skipper Lou "Skip-to-My-Lou" Clementine, Skip Lou for short.

I figured good news could mean only one thing.

"The bugs have bugged off?" I shouted with joy.

"Not exactly," Skip Lou admitted. "They're still there and the field's a total mess, but things aren't all bad."

"They've agreed to a trade to Lumleyville?" I joked. The Lumleyville Lumberjacks were one of the teams in our league. They were pretty good guys, but they couldn't play ball a lick. A big, scaly locust in the clean-up spot probably wouldn't hurt them. It might make them better, actually.

"Huh?" said Skip Lou. "Listen, I just got off the phone with Coach Burlap over in Hog City. He called to say their field is fine, no bugs in sight. We're on for tomorrow."

"Great," I said.

Playing our archrivals at their home field was kind of like getting a cavity filled. It wasn't exactly fun, but it was better than not having any teeth.

"He also offered to host the All-Star Game,"

continued Skip Lou. "Swell, huh?"

Swell? I thought. *Sure, it's swell. If by "swell" you mean lousy, no good, no fair, the Haymakers always get everything, this stinks like rotten eggs!*

What I actually said was "At their place?" Meanwhile, a hideous slideshow of Hog City Park packed to the rafters with obnoxious Haymaker fans flickered through my mind. The boos. The taunts. The cowbells.

"Pretty generous," Skip said brightly.

"But it's our game," I shouted. "We earned it! We won the pennant. It has to be here!"

We were planning to decorate the ball field with red, white, and blue bunting, just like the pros do. The school marching band was going to lead a parade to the field. Right before the first pitch, we would raise our championship banner. They couldn't take that away from us!

"Just an offer," Skip Lou soothed. "Maybe we won't need to take Coach Burlap up on it."

"Pray for wind," I said.

"Sure thing, Walloper," Skip said. "And remember, the bus leaves three thirty sharp tomorrow afternoon."

"See you then," I said, clicking off.

I went back to my room, sat down on the edge of my bed, and finished rolling gauzy white tape around the handle of my bat. I couldn't believe Hog City wanted to steal the All-Star Game from us, the weasels. We'd earned it fair and square! I would not let a bunch of bugs ruin things.

"We've got to hope this wind everyone's talking about does the trick, Mr. Bones," I said. "If it doesn't, we're going to have to take matters into our own hands!"

Mr. Bones looked up from where he lay at the foot of my bed, and I swear that dog smiled. You could tell he wanted nothing more than to take a run at the locusts.

When I had the bat just the way I liked it—a clean, grippy layer of tape stretching from the knob to six inches below the label—I put it aside and got my glove out from under my pillow.

31

I always sleep on my glove. It gives me good dreams. It also puts a nice hinge in the mitt.

I pulled off the thick rubber bands that held it closed and took the ball out of the pocket. Keeping a ball in the mitt and wrapping it with rubber bands helps shape the leather. The glove gets used to holding a ball. Then, come game time, it knows what to do.

I slipped my left hand inside the mitt and gave a few quick snaps. It clapped shut with the precision of a mousetrap. Perfect. That glove was ready to squeeze hot grounders like an alligator snaps up lunch.

A real alligator would've been nice. We could've sent it after the locusts. Assuming gators eat grasshoppers.

With my equipment in order, I went downstairs to the den and logged on to the computer. I wanted to find out as much as I could about our enemy.

Not the Haymakers. I already knew those guys inside and out.

I typed "migratory grasshopper" into the search box and hit return. Slingshot had mentioned the scientific name, but I couldn't remember it. I knew "migrate" meant to move from place to place. That seemed to describe the Rambletown bugs. What I wanted to know was how to get them going again. Away from Rambletown.

A second later I had about six gazillion hits. There must have been a website for practically every single grasshopper in the world. I clicked on a promising link and began reading. Almost immediately my skin started to crawl.

Here's what I learned:

1. Migratory grasshoppers are serious pests. They destroy wheat, vegetables, vines, bushes, trees, and grass.
2. When large outbreaks occur, the insects quickly exhaust food supplies. Then they take flight to look for fresh fields to munch.

3. The bugs swarm on clear, breezy days. With the wind at their backs, they fly at speeds of about ten miles per hour. They can cover sixty miles a day. Airplane pilots have encountered swarms flying as high as thirteen thousand feet above the ground.

4. You can use screens or cloth barriers to protect plants from grasshoppers. However, hungry grasshoppers can chew through most fabrics. If screens don't work, you can send chickens after them. Apparently chickens are bonkers for grasshoppers.

I clicked off the web page and shut down the computer. I didn't want to read any more. Chickens?! Rambletown Field was a ballpark, not a farmyard.

Plus, once the chickens got rid of the grasshoppers, how would we get rid of the chickens? It sounded too much like that song about the old lady who swallowed the fly. She eats a spider to catch the fly. Then she gulps a bird to get rid of the spider, chases the bird with a cat, and chokes down a dog to deal with the cat. Before you know it, half of Noah's Ark has slipped down her throat. And her chances of coming out alive do not look good.

Then again, neither did our chances of holding on to the All-Star Game if we didn't get rid of those grasshoppers.

★ CHAPTER 5 ★

ater that afternoon, Stump and Slingshot
showed up at my house. I knew they were
coming. We always got together the day after a
game to rehash the action. Between the grasshoppers and Stump's throwing error, we'd have
a lot to talk about.

But their arrival took Mr. Bones by surprise.

When the bell rang, he raced to the door
like a lifetime supply of dog treats waited on
the other side.

I opened up and he hurled himself onto the
porch, his tail wagging furiously as he jumped
up and licked my friends' faces.

The guys wore shorts and T-shirts and

carried their gloves. Their bikes lay in the driveway. I grabbed my mitt and a ball, and we went down to the front yard to play catch.

The grass was green and soft underfoot as we spread out, not a locust in sight. Apparently the bugs were still content with the smorgasbord down at Rambletown Field. They hadn't felt the need to branch out. A nice breeze chased clouds across a deep blue sky. The wind puffed steadily.

"So, Mr. Resident Insect Expert, what's your game plan?" I asked Slingshot. "For the Haymakers tomorrow, I mean. First we take care of the Haymakers, then we take care of the grasshoppers."

Pitching against the powerful Haymakers required only slightly more courage than fending off an army of mutant zombies. Those guys came at you relentlessly. If you messed up, they'd eat you alive. Kind of like the way the locusts were eating our field.

"Same plan as always," Slingshot said,

flipping the ball to Stump. "I just have to do my best and trust my stuff."

"Definitely," agreed Stump. "Trust your stuff." He caught the ball and zinged it to me.

"Yowch!" I yelped. "You trying to burn a hole in my hand or something?"

Stump smiled with satisfaction, his green eyes steely under the brim of his low-pulled cap.

I looped a lazy fly to Slingshot, who made a basket catch and kept the ball moving.

Stump gathered himself and whistled another hot one my way. For a friendly game of catch, he sure was firing bullets. I've eaten ballpark hot dogs with less mustard on them. And I happen to like mustard. Not to mention hot dogs.

"What's going on?" I demanded.

"Nothing. I'm just throwing."

"Hard enough to kill me," I said.

The next time around, Stump managed to put even more zip on the ball. Fortunately I caught it. If I'd missed, I think it would have punched a hole through the front of the house. The thing whizzed like a meteor.

A real meteor would have been nice. They say a huge one was what killed off the dinosaurs. A nice little space rock would take care of the grasshoppers.

"All right, that's it," I said. "Explain."

Stump dropped his head. "Sorry," he mumbled, kicking the grass. "I just need to know I still have it."

"Still have what?" Slingshot asked.

Stump sighed. "My arm. My throwing arm."

"Of course you do," I said. "You have a strong arm, and I have the sore hand to prove it."

"Wait a minute," Slingshot said. "Is this about what happened yesterday? Forget it! There was no error on the play. Bug invasion, remember? People were screaming. Everybody was already running off the field. No one was paying any attention to your throw."

"I was paying attention," said Stump quietly.

"I didn't even know about the swarm until after I fired the ball into the stands." He shook his head. "I can't get it out of my mind."

"You better get it out of your mind," I said. "We need to focus on the Haymakers."

We drifted back to the porch and sat down on the top step. Mr. Bones picked up the baseball in his mouth and cocked his head. He wanted to keep playing.

Stump was a great shortstop, always had been. He was like a one-man Bermuda Triangle. Balls hit his way just disappeared into his glove. Nobody covered more ground than he did. And nobody pulled the trigger quicker on a double play or got the ball faster to first.

"It happens," Stump insisted. "Haven't you ever heard of the yips? A guy wakes up one day and all of a sudden he can't hit the side of a barn. Nothing has changed—he does everything the same way he always has. Only difference is, now the guy stinks."

I'd heard of the yips, all right. The word was

slang for a mysterious twitchiness that some-times infected athletes, making them muff routine plays. The yips were a rare and terrible thing. They could crop up in any sport. If a bas-ketball player started bricking free throws he had always drained with his eyes closed, that was the yips. A golfer who suddenly could hit the ball anywhere except into the hole? The yips again.

But the yips were worst by far for baseball players. A yipified infielder turned every peg into an adventure. You never knew what the ball would do. The scary thing was, no one ever saw the yips coming. Or could predict when they would go away. Sometimes the condition disappeared as quickly as it arrived. Other times, it lingered all season . . . or longer. The harder a stricken player tried to get his groove back, the worse he would get. It was a sad and painful thing to see.

"Forget about the yips," Slingshot said. "One bad throw is not the yips. Besides, we've got the Haymakers to worry about. They're trouble enough."

"Not to mention locusts," I added. I brought up my conversation with Skip Lou. How he'd said the Haymakers were trying to use the grasshoppers as an excuse to steal the All-Star Game. *Our* All-Star Game.

Slingshot shook his head in disgust. "Why am I not surprised?" he asked, adding, "There's no way we're going to let that happen. We'll think of something." Stump didn't say a word. I'm not sure he even heard us. All he could think about was his error.

"You admit it was a lousy throw," he said.

"Drop it!" I said. "We need a new subject."

"Good idea." Slingshot agreed. "Let's take a rest from baseball."

Stump heard that.

He snapped to attention, eyes bugging so wide, you would have thought Slingshot had suggested we rob the Third National Bank or something crazy like that.

"What else is there?" he sputtered. His mind was like a monorail. It had only one track.

"Kites," I said. I told the guys about the plug for the Rambletown Kite Festival I'd heard on the radio that morning. I spoke quickly, so that Stump wouldn't cut me off before I finished. He was still trying to wrap his brain around the idea that it might be possible, now and then, to think about something other than baseball. "We should enter as a team," I concluded. "Get all the guys to do it."

"Great idea," Slingshot said.

"Whatever." Stump sighed.

I didn't say anything out loud, but I was thinking that aside from just being fun, the kite festival would be a good distraction for Stump. Help him blow off some steam before the All-Star Game. He really needed to lighten up.

"Only one problem," said Slingshot. "I don't have a kite."

"Got any money?"

He fished a black nylon wallet out of his

43

back pocket and looked inside. "Nine dollars in lawn-mowing cash. I spent the rest on the new Grand Slam Baseball for Gamebot 3000."

Stump perked up. "Good investment," he said of the computer game.

I pursed my lips. I didn't actually know how much a kite cost. There was only one way to find out.

"Let's ride down to the Toy Box. See what kind of selection they have."

"You need one, too?" Slingshot asked.

I was pretty sure we had an old kite in the garage somewhere. My family had picked it up at the beach a couple summers back. Looked like an owl. Every seagull on the beach had been terrified of it.

"I'm set," I said. "But it'll be fun to go anyway. I love that store. C'mon, we'll pick up Velcro on the way."

I opened the door, poked my head inside, and asked my mom if we could ride our bikes into town. She was cool with the plan.

"Be back in an hour," she said.

"Thanks, Mom," I said.

Stump, Slingshot, and I mounted our bikes and pedaled for town. Mr. Bones trotted alongside us, his tongue flapping in the breeze like a pink sock on a clothesline.

★ CHAPTER 6 ★

We swung by Velcro's house on our way to the Toy Box and found him in his yard fielding pop-ups off a pitchback.

Mr. Bones raced over and greeted him with his usual lick to the face.

"Pffft," said Velcro.

Slingshot glanced around. "Good thing you don't have a fence here," he teased. "Or did you knock it down already, chasing fly balls?"

"No pain, no gain." Velcro laughed.

Actually, he hadn't run into anything in weeks. If he kept it up, he was sure to make the All-Star team next year.

I told him we were on a mission to get kites

for the festival and asked if he could come.

He popped into the house to check with his mom and emerged a second later, flashing the thumbs-up sign.

The four of us jumped onto our bikes and rode the last half mile into the center of town, passing the library, the bank, a couple restaurants, and the hardware store. Along the way people waved and wished us luck in the All-Star Game. Holding up copies of the *Rambletown Bulletin*, a few shouted anxious questions about the locusts.

"Cross your fingers for wind," I called to them.

As if on cue, the breeze kicked up, unleashing a gust that tried to stop us in our tracks. I took it as a good omen. I hoped the grasshoppers over at the baseball field were paying attention.

The Toy Box occupied a skinny red brick building between a burrito place called Bueno y Sana and Serio's Market. We left Mr. Bones with our bikes on the sidewalk and went inside, a brass bell on the door announcing our arrival.

I inhaled the familiar wood-polish smell of the old shop with its scuffed floorboards and its narrow aisles, lined floor to ceiling with shelves loaded to bursting with board games, plush animals, magic kits, remote-control cars and airplanes, paint sets, balls, scooters, and model rockets. Man, I loved that place. I'd gotten my first bike there, and my first baseball bat and glove.

"Wow!" said Velcro. "I've been wondering what was in here."

"Pretty much every cool thing in the world," I said, picking up a Magic 8 Ball from a bin by the door. Suddenly I had an idea. "Hey, Stump," I said. "Ask it about the yips. This'll prove you're fine."

Stump grimaced. "I'd rather not," he said.

"Oh, c'mon," said Velcro. "I'll do it for you: Does Stump have the yips?"

As I turned over the ball to see the answer, the store owner walked up and greeted us. "Hi, guys. Anything I can help you find?"

I glanced at the white triangle floating in blue ink.

"Kites," I said decisively. "For the festival."

"Ahh," he said. "Everybody wants kites today. A fellow came in just a minute ago, looking for one. Right this way."

I dropped the Magic 8 Ball back into the bin, and we followed him down a jam-packed aisle.

"You boys ballplayers?" the owner asked. We told him we were. "I thought I recognized you. The kid in the back must be a friend of yours. Hey, what's going on down at the field? The pictures in the paper look horrible. How are you going to get rid of those pests before the big game Sunday?"

A step in front of me, Stump twitched, his right elbow nearly flicking over a Lego tower. "I hate those bugs," he muttered.

"There's a good chance the wind will blow them away," Velcro said, sounding more hopeful than convinced. "Right, Slingshot?"

Slingshot nodded.

We reached the sporting-goods section, and the man showed where to find the kites. We couldn't believe our eyes. Who knew there were so many different kinds? Along with standard diamonds, there were giant box kites, mile-long dragons, and kites designed to look like bats, birds, biplanes, comets, caped superheroes, and just about anything else you might possibly see in the sky.

A real superhero would have been nice. He could've rounded up the locusts for us.

Standing with his back to us, a tall kid wearing a baseball cap looked over a fabric replica of the *Star Wars* Death Star. He pulled the package off the hook and turned to take it to the counter.

When I saw his face, I stiffened.

He was no friend of ours. More like the exact opposite. Before us stood Flicker Pringle, all seven feet of him, star pitcher for the Hog City Haymakers. Unlike many of his teammates, Flicker was clean-shaven, but everything else about him was filthy. Especially his stuff. And his temper.

Flicker was famous for feeding hitters a starvation diet of nasty sliders, diving splitters, and heaters so fast they made a switchblade seem slow. That was when you could see his fastball at all. Usually you just heard a frightening *whoosh* as it rocketed under your chin. League leader in wins, strikeouts, and earned-run average, Flicker would be starting the All-Star Game. It would be strange to be on the same side as him.

"What's he doing?" Velcro hissed.

"Buying a kite, it looks like," I whispered. "Be cool. No big deal."

"Why, look who's here," Flicker sneered when he recognized us. "The Rambletown Grasshoppers!"

"Rounders," Stump corrected him. "The name's the Rounders."

He jiggled nervously as he spoke.

"Whatever," said Flicker. "Too bad about your field, huh? Don't worry, we'll put on a good All-Star Game in Hog City. *We're* used to it." Pushing past us to the counter, he added, "But first we'll kick your butts tomorrow."

"Dream on," said Slingshot.

Flicker ignored him as he paid for his kite. On his way out of the store, the Haymaker bully paused long enough to fire off one last shot. Fixing Stump with a cocky smirk, he asked, "What's up with your wing, pal? I hear it's dinged. Got you throwing like a crooked stick. Good luck with *that* in the All-Star Game."

"Sticks don't throw!" I called out lamely, but he'd already disappeared through the door.

Ugh!

So much for our fun little outing to the Toy Box. Stump practically vibrated, he was so upset.

The shop owner looked on in confusion. "Not a friend?" he asked.

"Not so much," Velcro said.

"Forget him," I said. "Let's get what we came for."

"I'm not in the mood anymore," Stump mumbled. "I'll wait for you guys outside." He stormed out of the shop.

"Maybe this was a bad idea," I said.

"Nah, he'll be fine once he cools down," Slingshot said. "I, for one, am still stoked about the festival. Help me find the biggest kite nine dollars can buy!"

After we looked over about a zillion options, Slingshot picked a diamond-shaped plastic one, black with a grinning skull and crossbones printed across its underside. Velcro found a giant red lobster whose long tail would swing freely as it flew. By the time they finished choosing, we felt pretty excited again. The festival would be a blast.

Almost as much fun as making Flicker Pringle eat his words tomorrow.

Thanking the owner, who wished us luck again in getting rid of the grasshoppers, we jingled out the door. We found Stump sitting on the sidewalk, back against the wall as he stroked

Mr. Bones, who sprawled across his lap.

"Any luck?" he asked.

Slingshot and Velcro showed him their kites. "Sweet," Stump said without much enthusiasm.

We mounted our bikes and headed home. With a building breeze pushing from behind, we practically coasted the whole way. Just before I split off, Stump called to me.

"Hey, Walloper," he asked. "What did the Magic 8 Ball say, anyway? You never told me."

Rats. I was hoping he'd forgotten.

"Magic 8 Ball?"

"Yeah, when you asked it about the yips."

"It's just a dumb toy," I said.

"I knew it!" Stump yelled. "It answered yes, didn't it?"

I shook my head. "It definitely didn't say that." I pedaled away before he could ask any more questions.

In fact, what the Magic 8 Ball had said was "Without a doubt!"

★ CHAPTER 7 ★

The next afternoon Stump and Slingshot swung by my house on their way to catch the team bus to our game against the Haymakers.

"We're in for a real blast of wind," said Mom. "You sure I can't give you boys a ride?"

I told her we wanted to take our bikes.

In fact I would've pedaled through a ring of fire before I accepted a lift. My mom knew this. Her offer wasn't really serious. More of a gentle tease than anything else. She knew how I felt about messing with tradition: only bad things could happen.

Things like striking out with the game on the line.

Or coming down with the yips.

I sure hoped the Magic 8 Ball was wrong about Stump. One way or another, we'd find out for sure today. The game would be the real test.

"Okay, then. Good luck, guys!" Mom appeared in the doorway. "I'll see you in the second inning."

My friends laughed. They knew my parents always showed up late, home or away. This was another long-standing tradition. Years ago, my folks happened to miss the start of one of my games after my dad misplaced the car keys. He was always forgetting where he put things. But that's another story. On the day in question, I ended up clobbering a ton of hits. Ever since then, Mom and Dad avoid the first inning of all Rounders games. They don't want to jinx me by being on time.

"Thanks, Mom. See you later," I said.

"Much later," said Slingshot with a laugh.

We rode to Rambletown Field together to meet the team bus for away games. It was a tradition. In baseball you don't mess with tradition.

We mounted our bikes and headed off to Rambletown Field. Mr. Bones dashed alongside us.

Everything looked normal as we pedaled into the parking lot.

Looks can be deceiving.

The first sign that something was wrong was the deafening roar that greeted us. It was no ordinary ballpark roar, the kind fans make when the home team does something good. Nope. Not even close. This sounded more like some terrible orchestra made up of chain saws, dirt bikes, and snowmobiles.

It was the grasshoppers.

Real snowmobiles would have been nice. They would have meant winter, when locusts don't swarm.

We sure hadn't seen any locusts last winter. Of course, we hadn't seen any grass, either. So much snow had fallen that the baseball diamond was still buried on opening day. Over at Rambletown Elementary School, snowplows had piled the white stuff into a jagged mountain in the parking lot. High up on the summit of it, the faces of four presidents had appeared as if by magic. Cross my heart and hope to die. We had John Adams, Calvin Coolidge, Franklin D. Roosevelt, and John F. Kennedy. And we didn't have a single locust. Presidents were way less obnoxious than grasshoppers.

Upon hearing the deafening buzz, my heart sank. I realized I'd been hoping that the grasshoppers would be gone.

We jumped off our bikes at the rack near the entrance to the field. The rest of the team was already aboard the bus. As I snapped my Kryptonite lock into place, Mr. Bones edged toward the diamond. By the way he moved, low to the ground, body-tense, I knew he planned to attack. Man, he hated those grasshoppers even more than I did.

Quickly I turned and whistled. We didn't

have time to mess with grasshoppers right now. Mr. Bones shot me a surprised look over his shoulder: "What?! You're just going the let them buzz around like they own the place?!"

"C'mon, boy," I encouraged him, flashing a big fake smile. "This way!"

Good dog that he is, he veered away from the field. You would have thought I had commanded him to go into a burning house to save a cat, the way he tucked his tail. I made a mental note to reward him with an extra treat when we got home after the game.

"Glad you boys could join us," Skip Lou said from behind the big wheel as we climbed into the bus. "I was beginning to think you had better things to do. Grab a seat and let's go."

Mumbling apologies for being *almost* late, we followed Mr. Bones down the aisle. Along the way, we slapped hands with our teammates.

Mr. Bones led us to the big bench seat all the way in the back, his favorite perch, and leaped up next to Gabby Hedron.

She had her notebook open on her knee and a camera looped around her neck on a black strap. Her brown ponytail stuck out the back of the red Rounders cap she wore. So much for the press not taking sides.

"Nice story in the paper," I told her. "I can't wait to read the one about the grasshoppers leaving."

"I hope we smoke them," Gabby said.

"Hey," Slingshot said. "That's not a bad idea! Maybe if we build a huge bonfire, the smoke will drive away the grasshoppers."

"I'm talking about the Haymakers," Gabby said. "The Haymakers totally bug me."

"Don't mention bugs," Stump groaned. "I'm sick of bugs."

Skip Lou cranked the bus into gear and we picked up the road to Hog City. The place lay only a short distance from Rambletown, but going there always felt like entering a different world.

The people of Hog City were loaded, and

their stuff was like a jumbo meal from Burger Clown. It was supersized. The huge brick houses, the park-sized lawns in front of them, the wide roads, the boss cars rolling over them: big and perfect and made to impress.

And then there were the baseball players. To a person, the Haymakers were gigantic. Every kid on the team looked like a grown man.

A big, bearded grown man.

That's right. Half these guys had facial hair.

You didn't often see a bunch of eleven-year-olds sporting chinstraps. But the Haymakers were no ordinary kids.

Think Paul Bunyan with a baseball bat instead of an ax and you begin to get the picture. Think Blackbeard the pirate. The Haymakers were so bristly, they could've opened a brush factory. And they could've used the brushes to tame their beards.

Now we were on our way to play them.

Lucky us.

"What's up, Stump?" Gabby suddenly asked.

"You're squirming all over the place."

"Worried about the game, I guess," he mumbled. "Sorry."

"You need to chill," Slingshot said. "We've beaten the Haymakers before. If I'm not mistaken, we're the champs. Hey, Gilly, how about some tunes?"

Gilly always brought his radio with him on bus trips. It was a big black box the size of my grandfather's suitcase. The thing could crank. You didn't even need earbuds to hear it.

Our first baseman grinned, and a second later the smooth voice of Louie the Lip filled the bus. I had to hand it to the Lip. The dude was a goofball, but his voice was butter. Whenever I heard it, I got hungry for popcorn.

My friends felt differently.

"Man!" said Kid Rabbit. "This is the worst station on earth! My parents listen to this junk!"

Out of nowhere a balled-up sock flew across the bus and lightly bounced off Gilly's ear. He only smiled more widely and jacked up the volume.

The Lip crooned:

"Let's go to the vault for a blustery classic by Ol' Blue Eyes himself. Because it's windy, windy, windy out there and it looks like it's going to stay that way for a while. Speaking of wind, the Rambletown Kite Club hosts its annual festival tomorrow at Rambletown Park. Be there or be square! Now here's Frank Sinatra doing 'Summer Wind.'"

"The music may stink," I said, "but you've got to admit the kite festival is cool. Stump, Slingshot, Velcro, and I are going after practice tomorrow. Who else is in?"

Everybody's hands shot up in the air.

Suddenly the bus gave a violent lurch. At first I thought Skip Lou had lost himself in the music. He loved old-time stuff. He'd been known to chair-dance to it while driving. But then I saw a clump of what looked like feathers flash past the windows.

"Was that chickens?" asked Gasser.

Gabby swiveled around and started snapping pictures through the rear window.

"I saw them, too," shouted second baseman Ellis "the Glove" Rodriguez, bouncing into the aisle for a better view.

"Stay in your seats," Skip Lou hollered as the bus lurched hard the other way and a polka-dotted bedsheet billowed past. "We're in for some turbulence."

"Isn't that what the pilot says right before the airplane crashes?" the Glove asked.

"Luckily this is a bus," Gabby said, still snapping away.

The guy on the radio sang about summer wind as more stuff flew through the air.

Leaves. Branches. Plastic grocery bags. Small animals.

A white shirt appeared out of nowhere and swam alongside the bus. A pair of blue jeans raced after it. Next came a flock of dark socks that dipped and weaved like sparrows. A small woman holding a large basket brought up the rear of the freaky parade. She gripped the basket in front of her with both hands like a steering wheel.

As she swooped beside the bus, our eyes met. She gave a little wave with her pinky finger, and then she was gone.

"That was weird," said Gasser, speaking for all of us.

We were still struggling to wrap our minds around what we'd seen when a roadside sign came into view. The sign bore raised gold letters set against a creamy white background. Firmly attached to a pair of thick wooden posts, it stood fast against the wind.

WELCOME TO HOG CITY
A COMMUNITY OF DISTINCTION

Instantly we erupted into a chorus of *oinks* and grunts. Our traditional salute upon entering our rivals' Richie Rich hometown.

The barnyard outburst fired up Mr. Bones. He put his front paws up on the window and howled like a wolf.

"Easy, boy." I laughed. "It's just a joke."

"The Haymakers are no joke!" shouted Ducks from the front. "Beat Hog City!"

We picked up his rallying cry, and a chant of "Beat Hog City!" rocked the bus as we rolled through town. Passing a golf course greener than a dollar bill, we entered Satchem Park, home of the Hog City municipal athletic fields.

Home of the mighty Haymakers.

★ CHAPTER 8 ★

The wind met us like the defensive line of the Chicago Bears as we clambered off the bus. We lowered our shoulders and shoved back. It took some doing, but eventually we forced our way out.

I looked around. I didn't see a single grasshopper. Of course there wouldn't be any. Nothing bad ever happened in Hog City. The ball field, only slightly grander than Yankee Stadium and flying just as many championship banners, lay directly in front of us. The grass looked perfect. As always.

Shaking my head, I moved toward the diamond amid a crowd of Haymaker fans.

Kids wearing baseball jerseys, grown-ups with little blue robot phones clipped behind their ears, and tough-looking nannies pushing strollers loaded with fat-faced toddlers streamed toward the ballpark. Every other person carried a big brass cowbell.

I fell in next to a chubby kid waving a Haymaker pennant. Or maybe the enormous pennant waved him. In the squall, it was like a kite and he was the tail.

"The ball should really carry today, huh?" I said, trying to be friendly. "I mean if this wind keeps up."

The kid stuck out his tongue and blew a wet raspberry. He couldn't have been more than six years old.

"Tough crowd," remarked Velcro, who was making his first trip to Hog City. He glanced around. "What's with all the cowbells?"

"It's a Hog City thing," I shrugged. "You'll see."

"You mean he'll hear," snorted Ocho, as we pushed toward the diamond.

Hog City baseball fans loved cowbells. They swung them like battle-axes at every game. Thank goodness they didn't have real battle-axes. Those people hated to lose at least as much as the actual players did. Probably more. They'd do anything to win. At the moment several of them, crowding in from behind, were trying to give me flat tires.

"Cut that out," I snapped, whirling around.

The pudgy kid with the pennant stopped short. He raised his face to mine and blew another raspberry. Several grown-ups reached out and fondly ruffled his blond hair, as if he'd just said something unbearably cute.

"You leave little Augie alone, you big bully!" someone shouted.

"Me!?" I cried. "I'm just trying to get to the field."

"Why bother?" another voice called. "We're going to pulverize you!"

I threw up my hands. You couldn't reason with a mob. Turning, I pressed forward with the Rounders.

Ten feet from the entrance, a woman jumped in front of us.

"Stop right there," she commanded, holding up her hand, palm out, like a cop directing traffic.

A real cop would have been nice. He could have gotten those obnoxious Haymaker fans off my heels.

Even if the woman hadn't planted herself directly in front of us, she would have been hard to miss. For one thing, rings the size of donuts encrusted her fingers. For another, she was attached by a pink leash to a large Afghan hound whose long, silky hair was done up with pink bows. I've seen beauty queens on TV who looked less stuck-up than that dog.

"What is it?" I asked. I wished I had remembered my sunglasses. Her bling blinded.

"That's far enough," she snapped. "You're scaring Princess Pinky Muffin." Her dog drew back its thin lips.

I couldn't tell if the hair on the dog's back

stood up because of the wind or because it meant to bite me. Despite the pretty little bows and ridiculous name, the animal didn't look especially sweet.

Neither did the owner.

"I understand you have bugs." The woman shuddered. "Your whole town is infested with them. Ours is a community of distinction. We won't have it overrun with vermin."

The way she said it made it sound like the vermin she was talking about walked on two legs.

"This is exactly why I can't stand this place," Gabby muttered. "Bunch of snobs."

"They're grasshoppers," I said, my face reddening. "It's not like we've got cooties or anything."

"Says you," snorted the woman.

Just then Mr. Bones bounced forward and tried to sniff the Afghan. In perfect imitation of her mistress, the animal sprang backward, her whole body quivering.

"AAAIIIEEE!" the lady screeched. "A rat! It's a rat! Someone do something!"

"You have rats in Hog City?!" I asked, snapping my head around.

"It's your rat," she accused bitterly. "You brought it with you. First insects, now rats." She pointed at Mr. Bones, whose long nose twitched as he inched closer to the goofy hound. Mr. Bones is a dog who likes to be petted and likes to lick faces. He does not easily accept rejection.

"That's no rat," I said, laughing. "That's Mr. Bones, my dog. Here, boy!" He leaped up and licked my face, then raced around the crowd three times before settling at my feet, mouth open and tongue lolling.

A few cowbells rang out.

"Dog," sniffed the woman. "What kind of dog? It doesn't look like any dog I ever saw."

"He's a . . . he's a . . ." In truth, I had no idea what kind of dog Mr. Bones was. He was an ordinary lovable mutt, was all.

Suddenly I felt a sharp poke in the ribs. I

wheeled around and there stood Gasser, his pointy elbow planted in my side. "Why, ma'am, he's a royal Oxford sniffing spaniel," the center fielder said. "Very noble lineage. Bred to sniff the food of kings. You know, for poison."

"Oh, of course! A royal Oxford sniffing spaniel. I should have recognized the breed at once." The woman crouched down and made kissy sounds at Mr. Bones, who lunged forward and planted a wet one right on her mouth.

"Pffft," she said.

"I couldn't agree more," said Gasser. "Now if you'll excuse us, we have a game to play." He tugged my arm and we hurried away to the diamond. I felt like I was going to burst, I was trying so hard not to laugh.

"Royal Oxford sniffing spaniel! How in the world did you come up with that?"

"I don't know," said Gasser with a snort. "Maybe because I live on Oxford Street. And look at Mr. Bones. His nose is as long as my arm."

"Don't listen, buddy," I said as we crossed

over to the visiting team's bench area on the third-base side. "It's a good nose."

To the steady snap of Haymaker pennants whipping in the breeze, we started getting loose for the game. The flags nearly drowned out the cowbells. Which really said something. Because the overall effect of the bells was somewhere between a cattle stampede in a Swiss meadow and a thousand fire alarms going off all at once.

Down at field level, the wind didn't gust quite so fiercely. Even so, we did not attempt any jumping jacks. We just couldn't risk it. We knew if we leaped too high, we'd launch ourselves into the air currents. Then there would be no telling where we might touch down again. Halfway to Kalamazoo, most likely.

I grabbed a ball and asked Stump if he wanted to get in a few practice throws.

"Sure," he agreed.

We spread apart for some soft toss. At least I did. Stump gunned the pill harder than long division. His throws sliced through the breeze like arrows. After each one, his arm did something funny. It twitched like a chicken wing.

Or maybe like a grasshopper wing.

"Relax," I told him. "We're going to treat these guys like an order of Chinese food. We're going to take them out!"

"Easy for you to say," he grunted. "You didn't blow yesterday's game."

"Get over it," I said. "Those guys sure would." I nodded toward our opponents across the diamond. "Check out Hoot Fewster. Think he'd let one bad throw bother him?"

Looking at Hog City's burly first baseman was kind of like seeing the ocean for the first time. The sheer vastness shocked you. The letters across his chest were so big, they probably could be seen from outer space.

"Hoot's never made a bad throw in his life," Stump said. "He's an All-Star, you know."

As we marveled at Hoot's bulk, the big guy plucked a can of soda from his personal cooler. The can must have been slick, because it slipped from his giant fingers and skittered down the dugout steps. Hoot pounced on it and gave it a good shake, I guess to teach it a lesson for running away.

Then Hoot opened the soda.

"Uh-oh," I said into my glove.

Instantly a foamy jet of brown liquid gushed like a geyser into his face. His baseball cap blew eight feet in the air. Roaring as if the soda had pulled a fast one, he crushed the can like a grape.

"So maybe he's not the sharpest blade in the drawer," Stump said. "But he's great at baseball."

"So are you," I replied. "You made the All-Star team, too."

"Don't remind me," he said. "I'm nervous enough about *today's* game."

Before I could answer, the ump pulled his mask over his face.

"PLAY BALL!" he barked into the howling gale.

★ CHAPTER 9 ★

As the visiting team, we batted first.

Our lead-off man, Ducks Bunion, clapped on a helmet and strode up to the plate. Stump picked up a bat and headed into the on-deck circle.

"Let's go, Ducks," the guys and I called from the bench. "Give it a ride!"

Out on the mound, ace Haymaker pitcher Flicker Pringle rolled his trademark toothpick from one side of his mouth to the other.

He started Ducks with a trademark fastball. At least I think he did. The pitcher whipped the old pill so hard, I didn't actually see anything. The ball whooshed like a steam engine as it cut through the breeze. Then came a firecracker *pop* as it slammed into the catcher's mitt. Next I heard a sharp yelp that sounded like when Mr. Bones got underfoot and I accidentally stepped on his paw.

The yelp came from the Haymakers' catcher, Hanky Burns.

It hurt to catch Flicker Pringle's wrecking-ball pitches. Even the toughest catchers could only take an inning or two of it. That old fire-baller ate them up like potato chips.

"STEE-RIKE ONE!" the umpire barked.

Flicker got the ball back and rolled that toothpick of his from side to side. I hated to see him do that. I knew from experience that he only flashed his toothpick when he felt good. And one thing and one thing only made Flicker feel good: striking out batters.

Two blazing pitches later, luckless Ducks trudged back to the bench, Flicker's first victim of the afternoon.

Out in the bleachers, rowdy fans taped a

red *K* to the wall. In baseball code, *K* stands for strikeout. Flicker had once notched seventeen of them in a single six-inning game. Not only that, but we were the team he had done it against. In the championship, no less. But that particular game didn't end so well for the Haymakers. I knocked a ball out of the park in my last at bat, winning the pennant with a walk-off tater.

I'll never forget the feeling.

Of course I won't ever forget all the times Flicker struck me out, either. Those memories stung like jellyfish. I hoped to avoid his tentacles today.

"Forget it," I told Ducks on my way out to take Stump's place in the on-deck circle. "You'll rip one next time."

Up at the plate, Stump knocked the dirt out of his spikes. Flicker wound up and delivered smoke.

Stump started to swing, but the umpire cut him off.

"STEE-RIKE ONE!" he roared.

In the stands the crowd started punching around a beach ball. Bad idea. The wind grabbed the brightly colored ball and instantly blew it clear out of the park.

"Hit one that way!" I called to Stump as Flicker delivered another frightening pitch.

Stump surprised us all by squaring up to bunt. It took courage to bunt against Flicker. Or lunacy. You might as well jump into the path of a bullet.

Stump managed to deflect the incoming projectile, a neat little trick that probably saved his life. But it didn't do much for his attempted bunt. The ball caromed wide down the first-base line.

"STEE-RIKE TWO!" the umpire hollered.

Expecting another fastball, Stump swung at the next pitch like the crack of dawn. He swung early.

Good idea.

Except crafty Flicker didn't fling a fastball.

He fooled Stump with a wicked changeup. The ball might as well have been trailing a parachute, it settled so gently into Hanky Burns's mitt.

"STEE-RIKE THREE, YOU'RE OUT!" honked the ump.

Stump dragged himself back to our dugout looking like a kid heading home from school with a bad report card. Another red *K* appeared in the bleachers. The fans out there must have been using superglue to stick them to the wall. Nothing else could have withstood the gusts.

"BATTER UP!" cried the ump.

That meant me.

I took my favorite Louisville Slugger from Billy, rubbed the batboy's head for luck, and strode to the plate. Flicker glowered down at me from up on the hill, that rotten splinter rolling from side to side in his mouth. Part of me wanted to knock it out with a scorching hit.

Another part of me just hoped to survive.

"Howdy, Walloper," the pitcher drawled as I

tapped the plate with my bat.

"Flicker." I nodded at him.

"Get ready to have your socks blown off," he said.

He could have been talking about the wind. It tugged at my uniform like it wanted to strip me down to my underwear. But Flicker didn't care about the wind. He meant *he* was going to blow my socks off. With his fastball.

"We'll see about that," I said.

The All-Star pitcher wound up and hurled a high hot one.

Whoosh went the pitch.

Pop went the ball.

"Yowch!" hollered poor Hanky Burns.

"STEE-RIKE ONE!" barked the ump.

I was in no position to argue. All I saw was a vapor trail.

From the bench, my teammates shouted encouragement. "One swing, Walloper! One is all it takes."

I banged down my helmet and cocked my

bat. Flicker kicked. I watched the ball roll off his fingertips, flat, straight, true.

Yes! I thought.

I swung.

CRACK!

The ball leaped off my bat like Mr. Bones springs off the sofa when it's time for a walk. Jackrabbit quick. Finding daylight between short and third, it settled into left field for a clean single.

Our bench exploded in cheers. You would have thought we had won the World Series, the way the guys hooted and hollered. Getting a simple hit off Flicker Pringle could have that effect. It happened so rarely, it felt like a major victory.

Velcro came up next.

"C'mon now, Velcro," I called from first. "Drive me home!"

Flicker would have none of it, though. Raging now, his eyes smoky and hot like the eyes of some kind of demon, he shifted into overdrive.

The ball flew from his hand in a blur.

"STEE-RIKE ONE!"

"STEE-RIKE TWO!"

"STEE-RIKE THREE!" the ump barked hoarsely, sounding like a Doberman with laryngitis.

The top of the first ended without a score.

To a steady chorus of cowbells, we grabbed our gloves and headed onto the field to play some defense. Our bats weren't working yet. I hoped our gloves would be.

After tossing a few blades of grass into the air to get a read on the breeze, Slingshot opened with a fastball. Goosed by a tailwind, the ball blew past the Haymaker leadoff batter for strike one. Slingshot threw two balls after that, then another strike. With the count even at two and two, he broke out one of his muddy boots. That's his name for a big, looping curveball that looks like it's going to break inside and settle over the corner of the plate.

I grinned when I saw it coming, because I

knew something about this pitch that batters never recognize until it's too late. The ball never breaks. It stays outside. Which, according to Slingshot's mom, is exactly where muddy boots belong.

The batter lunged and missed.

"STEE-RIKE THREE!" barked the ump. "YOU'RE OUT!"

The second guy up dropped a fly into shallow right field. Ocho would have caught it, but at the last instant a strong gust nudged the ball out of his reach. He plucked it off the grass and fired it to the Glove at second base, holding the runner to a single.

With one out and one on, Flicker Pringle came to bat. The crowd went bonkers. The stands sounded like the Salvation Army on Christmas Eve, so many bells rang. The fans knew, we all knew, that if there was one thing Flicker could do even better than throw the ball, it was hit the ball.

Slingshot stared in for the sign. Tugboat

flashed his index finger. Slingshot nodded, wound up, and delivered an inside fastball for strike one. Next came ball one, low, then another called strike.

Ahead in the count, Slingshot decided to play it safe. Rather than giving Flicker something good to hit, he tried to goad him into a swing by nibbling at the corners. Flicker refused to bite. Not even a tantalizing muddy boot could get him to wave. The ump called balls two, three, and four, and Flicker trotted down to first base with a walk.

When he got there, he stomped on Gilly's foot. "Oh, sorry," he growled as Gilly winced.

What came next was even worse.

★ CHAPTER 10 ★

With men on first and second and the wind ripping like a band saw, Slingshot kicked and delivered to the fourth Haymaker batter of the inning. The pumped-up goon got out ahead of the ball and chopped it weakly toward short.

Just what the doctor ordered, I thought, as Stump charged in to make the scoop: a perfect double-play grounder.

Stump fielded the ball cleanly. But as he turned to flip the ball to the Glove at second base, his right arm jerked like it had a case of the hiccups. The ball squirted away. By the time the Glove tracked it down, runners stood safely on every base.

"Heads-up out there," called Skip Lou from the bench.

The next batter wasted no time in pasting another hit directly at Stump. This time the shortstop played it on a bounce, picked it neatly from his glove, and gunned it to Tugboat to cut down the lead runner at home.

Only his throw never reached Tugboat's big pie plate.

It bounced six feet up the first-base line.

"SAFE!" roared the ump.

With the first run of the afternoon in the bank, the Hog City bench jeered Stump's error mercilessly.

"Shortstop's got a chicken arm!"

"He has ants in his pants!"

"More like grasshoppers! He's all jumpy."

Stump looked like he wanted to crawl under second base and hide. I called time to give him a minute to pull himself together. The Glove and Slingshot joined our huddle.

"Forget it," I said, draping my arm around

my friend's shoulders. "The wind grabbed it. New batter, new chance."

"That's right," encouraged Slingshot. "Couple quick outs, the inning is over and we're only down one."

Punching the pocket of his mitt, Stump nodded gamely.

When I got back to third base, I had company. Flicker Pringle now stood on the bag.

"Dude, that is the worst I have ever seen," the pitcher sneered.

"Worst what?" I bristled.

"Case of the yips," said Flicker. "Stick a fork in your shortstop, pal, because he is cooked."

"You scored one run," I said. "We'll get it back, easy."

"Going to be a lot more than one with old Yippie McYipperson in the middle," said Flicker.

"His name is Stump," I said coldly, eyes straight ahead.

"Way he plays," Flicker shot back, "it should be Chump!"

"He's an All-Star," I barked.

"Not on my team, he isn't," Flicker said smugly. "You better believe I'm not going to let any chicken-winged shortstop ruin my All-Star Game."

"Since when is it *your* game?" I muttered.

At the plate the Haymaker hitter ripped Slingshot's very next pitch into right field for a single, and Flicker jogged home with the game's second run.

After that, the wheels really came off.

More accurately, Stump's arm did.

He committed two wild throws in a row, and Hog City cleared the bases. By the time Ducks snagged a swirling pop fly in left field to end the inning, nine batters had come to the plate, Stump had notched four errors, and Hog City sat on a six-run lead.

The only thing wilder than Stump's arm was the weather. Clouds raced across the sky like clipper ships. Occasionally, something solid raced along with them. I swear I saw a whole set of patio furniture zip by—a table, four chairs, and a sun umbrella. A man dozed in one of the chairs.

"Whipping williwaws!" exclaimed Skip Lou as he sent Tugboat up to bat to start the second. "It's blowing cats and dogs! Try getting some air under a ball, and we'll see if something good happens."

Tugboat caught Flicker off guard by swinging at the first pitch. He popped the ball up and, just as Skip had hoped, the wind did the rest. It grabbed his short fly and carried it over the center fielder's head and all the way to the wall. Tugboat chugged into second with a stand-up double.

"No fair," Flicker complained loudly. "The wind took it!"

"There's a lot of things I can control, son," said the ump. "But weather isn't one of them. Batter up!"

Gilly stepped in and promptly lofted a ball to short left. The third baseman camped under it to make what looked like a sure out. But the ball never came down. It caught a fast-moving air current and abruptly darted toward center field. Turning three quick circles—kind of like Mr. Bones before he settles down for a nap—it dropped straight from the sky between bewildered fielders. Tugboat raced home and Gilly wound up on third with a wind-aided triple.

It wasn't a normal way to score, but at least we were on the board.

By now Flicker Pringle practically had smoke pouring from his ears. It definitely came off the fastballs he hurled past Slingshot.

"STEE-RIKE ONE!"

"STEE-RIKE TWO!"

"STEE-RIKE THREE!" barked the ump without coming up for air.

"YOWCH!" yelped Hanky Burns, who after an inning and a third of catching volcanic heat was just about done for the day.

Flicker rolled his toothpick around in his mouth, while out in the bleachers, the Hog City faithful managed to glue another *K* to the wall.

Ocho followed Slingshot to the plate. New batter, same old result: a swinging whiff.

With two outs Ocho sat down and the Glove took his place in the box. The scrappy second baseman swung three times, and three times the ball sped past him like an express train. Fans tried to paste up another *K*, but this time the wind was ready for them. It snatched their cardboard letter and sent it sailing.

We went to the bottom of the second with the score six to one in favor of our rivals.

Staked to a big lead, the Haymakers started clubbing for the fences. Hog City is like that. They like to do things big. Besides, after watching us, they knew any ball they hit in the air would be near impossible to catch.

Slingshot is no dummy, though. He saw what the Haymakers were trying to do and used their aggressive swings against them. Throwing a battery of off-speed pitches, he goaded them into one wild-swing miss after another.

The second, third, and fourth innings passed without either team scoring. In the fifth, Flicker Pringle cleared everything with a line drive that moved so fast, not even the wind could slow it down. Right fielder Ocho James never had a chance. We got the run back in the sixth on zigzagging flies by Gasser Phipps (who had replaced Velcro in center), Tugboat, and Gilly.

But that was all we scored.

"STEE-RIKE THREE!" bleated the ump as the Glove swung and missed for our third out, the game ending exactly as it had begun: with a Flicker Pringle comet.

The pitcher pumped his fist, while out in the stands the windburned Hog City faithful fed their collection of red *K*s to the squall. Sheets of cardboard swirled like confetti.

Final score: Hog City seven, Rambletown two.

★ CHAPTER 11 ★

Losing a game felt about as good as getting kicked in the teeth. Losing to the Haymakers felt worse. Like maybe getting kicked in the teeth by a horse with brick hooves.

Real bricks would have been nice. We could have used them to build a shelter from the wind.

As it was, we ducked into the dugout for our traditional postgame huddle. My cheeks stung like they'd been rubbed with sandpaper, they were so raw from the blow. My eyes watered and my nose ran. It reminded me of a corny joke my dad liked to tell.

Question: "Why was the kid called the upside-down boy?"

Answer: "Because his nose ran and his feet smelled!"

I was about to share the joke with Ducks, when Skip Lou clattered down the dugout steps to give his postgame pep talk.

"You guys should be proud," he said, tucking his clipboard under his arm. Behind him, clouds of dust swirled across the infield. "You played hard in really difficult conditions. Slingshot pitched a great game. We had lots of good at bats. Don't let the final score get you down. It's a long season and we can't expect to win them all. Especially not against a team as tough as the Haymakers."

Gabby scribbled his words in her notebook. I knew they'd find their way into her game report and that I'd read them in the paper in the morning. I wondered if Gabby noticed the one thing Skip left out of his speech. Namely Stump's tough day. What was there to say, really? When your shortstop commits four errors, the best thing to do is try to forget it.

I glanced over at Stump. Sitting by himself off to one side of the bench, he stared at the cement floor hard enough to crack it. While I watched, Mr. Bones jumped up next to him. My dog licked my friend's face like it was an ice-cream cone. Normally that will make anyone laugh. But Stump didn't even crack a smile.

I guess he really didn't want the attention, because he suddenly jabbed his elbow at Mr. Bones. The dog yelped and leaped out of the way.

I jumped up from the bench. Mr. Bones was just trying to be friendly. Everybody knew that. Stump had no right to take out his frustration on Mr. Bones.

"I'm sorry!" Stump exclaimed before I could say anything. He looked like a graveyard at midnight: spooked. "You know I would never touch Mr. Bones!"

"You just did," I pointed out.

My face burned. And not just from the wind. Everybody was staring at us.

"I didn't mean to!" Stump cried, flapping his right arm wildly.

"Stop doing that!" I shouted.

"I . . . I . . . I can't stop!" he said as his arm continued to jerk and jiggle like a hooked fish.

"What do you mean?" I asked.

"I've been trying to tell you," Stump cried. "My arm has a mind of its own!"

When he said that, all the air seemed to rush out of the dugout. None of us said a word. None of us moved a muscle. None of us breathed. The dugout suddenly felt like a coffin, tight and airless and perfectly still. The stillest place on earth in the middle of the windiest day on record.

It might have stayed that way forever. Except for one thing. Stump's right arm. It flung itself away from him as though it meant to leave his body for good. Then, like a dog reaching the end of its leash at a full sprint, it gave a mighty jerk and fell flat.

"I've got it bad," Stump whispered. "Real bad. I'll never be able to play in the All-Star Game!"

My jaw dropped. My heart dropped with it. Those bad throws he'd made hadn't been flukes. The wind hadn't taken him. He had a full-blown case of the yips, for sure. I'd heard stories about the yips actually taking over a player's arm. Making it twitch like a dog with fleas. But I'd always thought they were urban legends. Now I knew it really could happen. My anger turned to dread. There was no known cure for the yips.

"Of course you'll play in the All-Star Game," said Skip Lou. "Everybody muffs a throw now and then. It's nothing to get all upset about."

He meant to be comforting, but I could tell Stump didn't buy it. I didn't either.

Probably better than anyone, I understood how Stump felt. Once I'd fallen into a hitting slump so deep and dark, it made Carlsbad Caverns seem bright. Carlsbad Caverns is a series of deep caves in the state of New Mexico. They plunge hundreds of feet below the earth and stretch for miles and miles in every direction. They're also full of bats. Compared to that slump I had, or to Stump's case of the yips, those caves are sunny.

Forget about locusts and crazy wind. The number one thing we needed to worry about was Stump. We had to find a way to cure him.

And we had to do it fast.

Before the All-Star Game.

The only question was . . . how?

We filed out of the dugout and onto the bus. From time to time during the ride home, a gust of wind tried to push the bus off the road. A cow or two sailed past the windows. But we all were too gloomy to pay much attention.

Stump, Slingshot, and I sat in our usual places in the back. Mr. Bones curled next to Stump, his head resting in Stump's lap. Mr. Bones is not the type to hold grudges.

Gabby finally broke the silence.

"Stump," she said softly, "I hate to bring it up, but I'm going to have to mention your game in my story."

"It doesn't matter," Stump said dejectedly.

"Write what you saw."

"Nothing personal, you know. If you don't mind, I'd rather just leave the yips out of it. It doesn't seem right to go there."

"To me it looked like the wind," I said. "Gave everyone fits today. The ball did crazy things."

"Definitely," Gabby said.

Stump started to say something, but I cut him off.

"You saw how those fly balls behaved," I said firmly. "It was the wind, all right."

Gabby nodded.

We said no more on the subject.

The minute Skip Lou pulled up at Rambletown Field and cranked open the door, everybody cleared out of the bus. Nobody said anything, but I could tell the guys wanted to put some distance between themselves and Stump. Fast. Nothing like the yips to kill a party. Not that the game or ride home had been much of a party.

More like a funeral.

Picking our way around branches downed by the storm, Stump, Slingshot, and I went to get our bikes. The wind hammered less forcefully than before. When I turned my back to it, my ears didn't get folded into origami.

The yips weighed so heavily on my mind that it took me a minute to notice that more than the wind had quieted.

"Hey," I said. "You guys hear that?"

My friends cocked their heads and listened.

"I don't hear anything," Slingshot said after a few seconds.

"Exactly," I agreed. "The buzz is much fainter."

We jumped onto our bikes and rode onto the diamond to have a look around. Mr. Bones charged ahead of us. He must have thought he was finally going to get a shot at those critters.

"Whoa!" Slingshot whistled as we wheeled toward the mound, which the wind had lowered by a good three inches. The whole field looked like it had been run through a blender.

Grasshoppers had torn the turf to smither-eens. Sections of outfield wall lay toppled by the storm. Beyond the field, in Rambletown Park, uprooted trees sprawled every which way, their branches tangled like the tentacles of giant squids spit out by the sea.

"Three days until the All-Star Game," Sling-shot said.

"The grass will never grow back in time," Stump said. "Not that I'll be playing. Grass or no grass."

From the distance came a familiar whine.

Slingshot nodded toward a cluster of large trees still standing beyond the ruined wall. Packed tightly together, they'd shielded one another from the storm and survived without damage.

"It's coming from there," he said. "The wind must have picked up the grasshoppers and swept them into those trees."

"Think they'll come back to the field?" I asked.

"Not unless the wind changes direction," Slingshot said. "Even if it did, there's not much left for them here."

Mr. Bones ran barking around the dirt. Dust puffed up at his every step. The diamond looked more like a giant sandbox than a place to play ball.

"They're gone, boy!" I called. "Come on, let's get out of here."

With that, we turned our bikes into the breeze and headed for home. When we reached our block, Stump and Slingshot peeled off one way, and Mr. Bones and I went the other.

"See you guys tomorrow," I said.

Slingshot waved.

Stump did, too.

At least I think he did. His arm definitely fluttered. But for all I knew, it might have been the yips.

★ CHAPTER 12 ★

"Mom," I called when Mr. Bones and I came through the door, "I'll get my own supper."

Rattled as I felt, only one thing would help. Fried-baloney sandwiches. When things go bad, there's nothing better to eat. Somehow, they make you feel better.

Without bothering to change out of my uniform, I dropped a fat pat of butter into a frying pan. Parking himself at my feet, Mr. Bones licked his lips. He knew what was coming. That's one thing about dogs. They're very sensitive to people's moods. Not to mention the smell of good stuff cooking.

I placed four slices of Old Leadbelly Sinker

bread in the melted butter and layered baloney on top of them. The butter sizzled. The baloney curled at the edges.

Mom came into the kitchen, took one look at the smoke, and said, "Tough game, huh? I still can't get over that hit of Gilly's, the way the ball turned cartwheels like that."

"It's more than the game," I said. "Stump has the yips, locusts have eaten our ball field, and the Haymakers are trying to steal the All-Star Game. Plus some hoity-toity Hog City lady called Mr. Bones a rat."

"Ouch," she said. She kissed my cheek. Then she leaned down and patted Mr. Bones. "Can I help?"

"Sure," I said. "You know a cure for the yips, how to make grass sprout overnight, and the secret to hitting a baseball in a gale?"

"With your meal, I mean."

"Fried baloney I can handle."

When the sandwiches were brown on one side, I flipped them over with a spatula and toasted the other. In no time at all, I had a nice heaping platter of them. Mr. Bones, meanwhile, had a serious case of the grumbles. His stomach bleated and burbled like a tuba packed with bubble gum.

A real tuba would have been nice. It would have drowned out the locusts I could still hear buzzing in my head.

I flipped off the heat and carried the sandwiches to the table. Mom poured a glass of milk and set it down at my place. Tail wagging to beat the band—and stomach grumbling just like a band—Mr. Bones camped beside my chair.

Then we started eating. A fried baloney sandwich for me, a fried baloney sandwich for Mr. Bones.

"Would you like one?" I asked Mom between bites. She didn't look exactly hungry. Astonished was probably a better description. Or maybe grossed out. But you never knew. "Plenty to go around."

"I'll wait for your father to get home," she

said. "We'll have something later. I mean lighter. We'll eat something lighter, later."

Nodding, I snarfed down another sandwich.

As I chewed, the door burst open and a gust of wind swept into the house. Dad blew in with it. His tie, the one printed with golf balls instead of fishing lures, wrapped his neck like a scarf, and his face glowed like he'd been sandblasted.

"Holy cow," he panted, pressing his back against the door and forcing it shut. "I've never seen anything like it."

"He couldn't help it!" I snapped.

"Who couldn't help what?" Dad asked.

"Stump," I said. "He didn't mean to throw away the game."

"Oh, yeah, that was tough. Poor kid! But I'm talking about the weather. I went back to the office after the game. You know the Maple Street bridge?"

I nodded.

"Well, it's the Elm Street bridge now. The wind pushed it three blocks south. Traffic is snarled for miles."

He plopped into a chair and noticed my stack of sandwiches, much smaller now.

"That bad?"

"The worst," I confirmed.

Mom quietly joined us at the table. She and Dad exchanged glances.

"The yips, huh?" Dad sighed. "When I was a kid, our second baseman came down with a nasty case."

"He did?"

"His aim got so bad, we had to close down the bleachers behind first base. Way too dangerous for people to sit anywhere in his line of fire."

"Yikes!" I said. Hopefully we wouldn't have to do the same because of Stump.

"Tell me this," Dad asked. "Has he reached the twitching point yet?"

Remembering the crazy way Stump's arm jiggled, I nodded. "Scary twitchy."

"Yep, sounds like Flapdoodle Flanagan all over again," Dad said. "Not his real name, of course. We called him Flash for the longest time. Kid had tremendous speed. Then his arm started jerking like a chicken wing, and some wise guy dubbed him Flapdoodle. Unfortunately it stuck. Eventually Flapdoodle got so discouraged, he quit baseball and joined the swim team."

"The swim team!" I cried. I couldn't imagine Stump ever giving up baseball. He loved the game too much.

"Turned out Flapdoodle moved even faster in water than on dry ground. Plus, his right arm worked like a bionic paddle. For each stroke everyone else made, he completed three. Of course, he could only swim in circles. If pools were round instead of rectangular, he could've been an Olympic champion."

"That's a terrible story!" I grimaced. "Didn't he ever get better?"

"The thing is, the yips only affected Flapdoodle when he felt nervous. During a tense baseball game, say, or at a swim meet. The rest of the time, he was rock solid. His hands were so steady, he became a surgeon when he grew up. Operating on people didn't make him nervous at all."

"See?" Said Mom. "There's hope for Stump yet."

Sure there was. If he wanted to be a doctor. Which I knew for a fact he didn't. Not a doctor, a concert pianist, or, for that matter, a professional juggler. Stump loved to play ball, pure and simple. Baseball was his life.

Still, my dad's story gave me plenty to think about. Such as the connection between the yips and nerves. So what was making him nervous?

That was the million-dollar question.

If we could answer it, I was sure we could help Stump beat the yips.

The wind?

I didn't think so. Stump's arm had started acting up before the weather went haywire.

The grasshoppers? I thought back to his first error, the one that started everything. It had happened during the game against St. Joe.

Tugboat had just spotted the locusts and called time. Immediately after, Stump had hurled the ball into the grandstand. Ever since then, he'd been wilder than the Amazon rain forest.

Maybe the bugs had spooked Stump more than he let on. He claimed he hadn't seen them until after he threw the ball. But what if he had caught a quick glimpse as he set up to throw? The shock of it certainly could have messed up his timing. Once the ball sailed away, his nerves took over. Baseball was everything to Stump. The idea of failing at it would have shaken him badly, especially with the All-Star Game only a couple days away. In that case, the grasshoppers could have been sort of a—whatchamacallit? A Trojan horse.

We'd learned about the Trojan horse in school.

A long time ago, the ancient Greeks fought a war against the kingdom of Troy. The Trojans retreated within the walled city of Troy and held off the Greek army for ten years. Finally the Greeks came up with a trick to end the war. They built a giant wooden horse on wheels, rolled the horse right up to the city gates, and pretended to go home. When the Trojans saw the statue, they figured it was a victory present. Who knows? I guess people really liked giant wooden horses back then. Anyway, feeling all smug, the Trojans pulled the statue into the city. Whereupon a band of Greek warriors sprang out from a secret compartment in its belly and took over the city. War over.

Maybe the grasshoppers were something like the Trojan horse. Instead of Greek soldiers, they carried fear and doubt. When the locusts swooped down, triggering Stump's error, they unleashed a storm of doubt in his mind. The more he worried, the worse he threw; the worse he threw, the more he worried. Around and around it went, like a merry-go-round. Except it wasn't merry. It was horrible.

My theory was rough. I'd need to work out the details. But it seemed to hold some promise.

If I was right, the way to fix Stump would be to knock the fear out of him. Send it packing with the grasshoppers.

Before going to bed that night, I picked up the phone and called Slingshot.

"Slingshot, it's me. Remember when I had my slump?"

"Who could forget? You struck out, like, thirty-seven times in a row."

"Yeah, well, you know how you guys woke me up in the middle of the night and did all that hocus-pocus stuff to cure me?" Even now, a year later, I could still taste the nasty potion they'd made me drink.

"Sure," said Slingshot. "The magic was make-believe, but the show we put on made the guys feel better. They thought you were cured, and that gave them the confidence we needed to beat the Haymakers and win the pennant."

"Exactly," I said. "I think we should do the same thing for Stump."

"Force-feed him a concoction of red pepper

flakes, milk, and foot powder?"

"I wouldn't go that far. But we need to do something startling, something that will shock him out of the yips." I explained my idea about the Trojan horse. Then I outlined my plan.

When I finished, Slingshot didn't say anything for a moment.

"Hello?" I said.

"Walloper," he breathed at last. "It just might work. Either that or he'll drop dead on the spot! If you can get the green light from Stump's parents, I'll take care of the rest."

"Deal," I said.

"When do we go for it?"

"Night before the All-Star Game," I said.

"I'll get right to work on the design," Slingshot said by way of saying good-bye.

He clicked off.

I punched in Stump's number. I hoped his mom or dad would answer.

★ CHAPTER 13 ★

Clouds drag-raced across the sky the next morning. Treetops swayed like hula dancers. I ducked back into the house with the paper and gave the weather report to Mom and Dad:

"A hurricane without rain."

Mom clucked sympathetically. Dad snorted.

"Go fly a kite!" he said.

"No," I said. "I'm serious. It's blowing like crazy."

"That's what I mean," he said. "Perfect kite weather!"

Right! The Rambletown Kite Festival. I'd almost forgotten. Today was the day. I hoped the distraction would be good for Stump. Take his mind off the yips for a bit.

"Could I take that old kite of ours to the festival after practice?"

"I don't see why not," Mom said.

"I wish I could go, too," Dad said. "Too bad I have to work."

We sat down for breakfast. Over a bowl of Pirate Crunch, I flipped through the inky newspaper to see what Gabby had written.

A photograph of Stump leaped off the first sports page. It showed him fumbling away the ball against the Haymakers. Ouch. Not the kind of picture you want in the paper.

Gabby's caption helped ease the pain:

Rambletown's All-Star shortstop Stump Plumwhiff commits a rare error against the Haymakers yesterday. Gale-like conditions made play difficult.

"Thank you, Gabby," I said aloud. She'd called Stump an All-Star, noted that he didn't usually make errors, and indirectly blamed the weather. Most important, she'd left the yips out of it, just as she'd said she would.

After finishing the paper and breakfast, I went into the garage and rummaged around for the kite. I found it tucked away on a shelf behind a bunch of empty flowerpots: a yellow nylon owl with two big black eyes, just as I remembered. Wound on a red spool, the string appeared to be in good shape. I hoped it was. The way the wind screamed, piano wire probably would've been a good bet.

I wrapped the kite around the top metal tube of my bike frame, tied it in place with its own string, then grabbed my mitt and pedaled through a strong headwind to Rambletown Field for practice. As he always did, Mr. Bones trotted along beside me.

When we got to the ballpark, I saw right away that the grasshoppers had not returned to the field. They were still camped in the same grove of trees where we'd seen them the night before. That was the good news.

The rest of it was bad.

The toppled sections of outfield wall had not righted themselves. No grass had magically sprouted. The field looked more like my uncle Harry the time his dog mistook his toupee for a chew toy and ran off with it. Bald. Completely bald. Out beyond the damaged fence, a crew of city workers wearing hard hats and orange vests cleared downed tree limbs.

As I surveyed the mess, the rest of the guys arrived for practice. One by one, they nodded my way. Billy Wishes even tried to wink. At least I think he did. It looked like he had something stuck in his eye. I took it to mean Slingshot had spread the word about my plan.

Skip Lou walked onto what was left of the field, carrying three big blue plastic buckets.

Mr. Bones poked his snout into one of the buckets. I don't know what he expected to find. Grass seed, maybe. But the buckets were empty. He looked at me. I looked at Skip Lou.

"We're going to try a little game," Skip Lou explained. "First let's run through our usual routine." He blew his whistle, signaling the start of practice.

The guys and I quickly formed a double line at home plate. Skip Lou had trained us well. We knew the drill. He gave another blast, and Ocho and Ducks took off on a fast lap around the diamond. We always started practice by running the bases.

Stump and I went next. We crossed first base and made the big turn toward second, Stump chugging along on the inside, I to his right. The Glove and Velcro breathed down our necks a few steps back. We ran like undercooked eggs to stay ahead of those two speed merchants.

Without any grass it was hard to tell where the base paths ended and the field began. The diamond looked like one big mud puddle waiting to happen. I hoped the wacky weather forecast didn't include rain.

"You got your picture in the paper," I puffed as we crossed second in a cloud of wind-whipped dust.

"Yep," Stump said, digging for third.

I didn't press him for an opinion.

"How's the wing?" I puffed. "Any better?"

"Wing's not hurt. Just won't work."

As we rounded the bag, he elbowed me hard in the ribs and darted away. I caught up and he jostled me into foul territory.

"Quit it," I said. "Just warming up. No points for finishing first."

Stump batted me again.

A real bat would have been nice. The flying kind. They eat insects. Maybe a flock of them would devour the grasshoppers, which had started droning again in the trees where they roosted.

"Quit what?" Stump puffed.

"Quit . . . oh! Never mind!" I got it. The yips struck again! I swung wide to avoid his flailing elbow.

We crossed the plate stride for stride, then joined Ducks and Ocho at the backstop to urge on the guys still running. Not that we could actually see anyone. Stirred up by our footfalls and the steady gale, a dust storm had completely engulfed the diamond. I couldn't make out much of anything more than three feet in front of my face.

"Holy smokes!" Ducks exclaimed.

"Thicker than any smoke I ever saw." I blinked.

As we stared, first the Glove, then Velcro emerged from the gritty brown cloud. One after another, the rest of our teammates stumbled out behind them. Caked in grime, they looked as if they'd just crossed the Sahara Desert. Any second now, I expected camels to appear.

Real camels would've been nice. They have long eyelashes to protect themselves from sandstorms.

Right then and there, Skip Lou decided to move practice off the diamond.

"This is ridiculous," he snorted. "Follow me."

We gathered up our stuff and trudged out of our sand pit. It felt good to breathe clean air again. Not to mention being able to see.

Slingshot fell in beside me.

"Did you get the green light from Stump's parents?" he whispered.

I checked over my shoulder. Stump moped along by himself at the back of the pack.

I nodded.

"Excellent," he said. "I'll get the supplies after practice. Everybody's coming to my house tonight to make what we talked about."

Suddenly Mr. Bones let out a yelp and ran toward the buzzing trees. Launching himself through the air, he scrabbled three feet straight up the nearest trunk before gravity pulled him back to earth. He turned a back flip and landed on his feet. For a second the bugs fell silent. Then they started up with the horror music again, even louder than before.

"That dog should be in a circus!" One of the workers laughed.

A real circus would've been nice. They always stretch huge nets beneath the high wire. We could've used nets to catch the locusts. Mr.

Bones sure didn't have any success. I called him away from the trees.

"Is he smiling?" Gasser asked as Mr. Bones trotted over to us. "He looks like the cat who swallowed the canary. If I didn't know better, I'd say he has something up his sleeve."

"Except he doesn't have sleeves," I said.

"Whatever did happen to that coat he used to wear?" Velcro asked. "You know, the plaid one?"

"Ugh," I said, remembering the horrible little doggy jacket Mr. Bones had gotten for Christmas. The thing made him look ridiculous, like a throw pillow with a head sticking out one end and a tail wagging at the other. He'd proudly worn it all winter long. "Don't mention the coat," I said. "He'll want it back."

Skip Lou led us to an open area at the edge of the Rambletown Park playground. Telling us to hang tight for a minute, he went over and talked to the leader of the work crew. The conversation involved a lot of nodding and pointing.

As they spoke, we watched a steady stream of

cars pull into Rambletown Park. People jumped out, carrying bags and boxes, and headed for a large open area a few hundred yards beyond the playground.

Tugboat squinted his eagle eyes. His face brightened. "Kites," he said. "They're setting up for the festival!"

"I brought mine!" the Glove announced. He unfurled a gray-blue kite in the shape of a shark. "Anybody else?"

"Tied to my bike," I said.

The other guys nodded. Almost all of us had remembered kites.

Before we could say anything more, Skip Lou returned and proceeded to arrange the blue buckets in a row on the wood chips about fifteen feet from where we stood.

He turned and faced us.

"Listen up, guys," Skip Lou said. "We're going to break into two teams to practice throwing. Never hurts to work on accuracy."

He didn't mention any names. He didn't need to.

★ CHAPTER 14 ★

"The game is called bucket ball, and the rules are simple," Skip said. "Each player gets six throws. You score one point for hitting a bucket, two for landing a ball inside. Hit all three buckets twice and you pick up five bonus points for your team. I deliberately set the buckets close. At this distance, the wind shouldn't be much of a factor. Winners earn bragging rights. Everybody else gets to run."

We all snapped to attention. Skip Lou often devised competitive drills for practice. The squad that came up short always ran. The Losers' Lap, we called it.

We chose sides. Ducks, Gilly, the Glove, Ocho,

Kid Rabbit, and Tugboat formed one team. They were the Reds. Slingshot, Gasser, Velcro, Stump, and I made up the Blues. We had Slingshot, so they got the extra man. With his accuracy, the pitcher was worth at least two players.

To keep things fair, the Reds got to pick which of our players would take two turns. They huddled to compare notes. The obvious choice would be Stump. I wondered if they'd be low down enough to make it.

After a few seconds of whispering, the five of them straightened. Ocho cleared his throat.

"Gasser goes twice," he said, his teammates nodding behind him. "He can take twelve throws in a row or two turns of six."

We all knew they'd given us a break.

"Hear that, Gasser?" Skip grinned. "These guys think you can't hit the side of a barn!"

"We'll see about that." The center fielder laughed.

For his part, Stump didn't say anything. His expression spoke louder than words, though.

He looked like an elephant had just climbed off his back.

Kid Rabbit got things going for the Blues. In six tries he nailed two targets and neatly dropped one ball into a third. Four points—a very good start. Gasser stepped up for us. Electing to use all his tosses at once, he plunked three buckets on his first go-round and five more on his second.

"There's your barn," he said smugly.

Because Gasser counted for two turns, the Reds sent up a couple players in a row. Gilly drilled three of six, just missing a two-pointer when his last attempt rimmed out. Ocho followed him and rallied his side into the lead by scoring four times.

Taking the ball with the Reds up 11–8, Slingshot put on a clinic. He scored on all six of his throws, including a high-arching eephus pitch that settled in for two. The five bonus points pushed his score to twelve and gave us a total of twenty.

Throwing for the Reds, Tugboat rifled the ball like he meant to cut down a base runner trying to steal second. It would have taken more than wind to knock his cannon shots off course. His first three blasts nailed their marks dead center, sending the buckets flying. After Skip reset them, Tugboat took deadly aim and toppled two more. His sixth attempt sailed a fraction of an inch high. Lucky for the bucket. Lucky for us, too: no bonus for the Reds. Velcro came up next and gave us three out of six, each of his misses narrower than the edge of a dime.

Ducks grabbed the ball from him and took aim for the Reds. Lobbing gentle rainbows, he dropped six balls in a row into the buckets. Amazing! Twelve points plus the bonus of five gave those guys a whopping total of thirty-three. Even though Ducks had stolen the lead, we all cheered his incredible performance. You've got to admire perfection.

"There's your All-Star left fielder!" Skip hollered as Ducks beamed and we all clapped like mad. "Way to go, kid! What touch!"

Having carefully watched four and a half rounds, I decided to try for straight pegs on my turn. We were down 33–23 and we flat out needed some hits. I figured it made sense to go after the easy points rather than to chase the tricky ones. Concentrating hard, I picked off the buckets one after another—*plink, plonk, plunk*—and pocketed the bonus. Eleven points gave us thirty-four. More important, it gave us the lead again.

For a few seconds, it did.

I handed off to the Glove, who promptly nailed half his chances. Down to our last man, we now trailed the Reds by 36–34. Only one player stood between them and victory.

The player was Stump. He needed two hits to tie, three to win.

I held my breath as he took aim at the bucket on the right.

Stump reached back and fired a dart. Straight and true, the ball met plastic and made a beautiful *thunk*.

"Way to go, Stump!" I roared, slapping high fives with the Blues. He'd cut the Reds' lead down to a single point and still had five shots left. Things looked good. Stump looked even better. He looked like he'd beaten the yips!

As he gathered himself for his second shot, a strong gust of wind blasted through the park. It must have disturbed the grasshoppers, because all of a sudden they started buzzing louder than ever. It definitely disturbed Stump. His arm hiccuped and the ball bounced wide of the mark.

Four shots to go.

"Nice and easy now," called Gasser.

Stump nodded. The grasshoppers whined. He threw. The ball fell short. Three shots to go.

His next one sent Mr. Bones scrambling for cover.

We winced.

"Just toss it like you always do," I called. "Nothing to it."

He tossed the ball, all right. He tossed it

131

smack off the side of the climbing structure in the middle of the playground. The grasshoppers seemed to get a kick out of that. Their chirping sounded like laughter.

One shot left. Stump needed to make it count to tie the game. Judging by the way his arm twitched, what he really needed was a miracle.

We tried to drown out the bugs by cheering. Everybody joined in, Reds and Blues alike. Forget the score. Stump was our friend. He was our teammate. We hated to see him struggle. All of us pulled desperately for him.

And he tried. You could see how hard he tried. He took a deep breath. His right arm drew back, and the left reached forward and pointed at the target. It all looked textbook . . . right up to the end. Just as he released the ball, a horrible shiver ran through his body. A twitch, a jolt, a jerk, a stammer. The yips. He fired the ball into the ground like he meant to bury it.

Our cheers died in our throats. We looked away. It was probably the worst throw any of us had ever seen in our lives.

Skip Lou kept quiet. He just circled his finger in the air.

Slingshot, Gasser, Velcro, Stump, and I took off on the Losers' Lap. We kept quiet, too. We had nothing to say. As we jogged around the playground, only our footsteps and steady breathing disturbed the uneasy silence. That and grasshoppers droning in windswept trees.

★ CHAPTER 15 ★

When we finished the Loser's Lap, Skip tried to run some batting practice. But nobody had much heart for it. Between the yips and the kite festival, now in full swing across the park, we couldn't concentrate. After a while he made like the sunset and called it a day.

"Pack it in, fellows," he said. "I can see your minds are elsewhere. Let's meet back here first thing tomorrow morning. We'll see if we can get the field in any kind of shape for the All-Star Game. In the meantime, go and try to have some fun."

With that we grabbed our kites and took off across the park, where flying objects of every size, shape, and color painted the sky like a rainbow. Bat kites, bird kites, butterfly kites, box kites as big as refrigerators, traditional diamond-shaped kites sporting hot colors and long, streaming tails. Snarling red-and-gold Chinese dragons, silver flying saucers, stunt kites, stacking kites. Kites cut to look like biplanes and pirate ships, octopuses and sting-rays, puppy dogs and polar bears—all soaring among the high-flying clouds.

Down on the ground, a huge crowd milled about gawking, eating, and swaying to the loud music that thumped from a white tent embla-zoned with the logo of the radio station WHOT 102.5. Some vendors peddled fried dough from red-and-white-striped carts. Others sold hamburgers, and hot dogs sizzled on a grill. Souvenir sellers hawked T-shirts and bumper stickers. Kids wrestled on the ground, dogs barked, the wind raced.

Flicker Pringle was there, too, flying his Death Star high overhead.

Eager to launch, I handed my winder to Stump. "Let out some line," I told him, backing away with the kite. He hadn't brought one of his own. As rattled as he looked after bucket ball, I wanted to rope him in to the fun.

He nodded and peeled off twenty feet of string.

"Run!" I said, taking up the slack. He charged into the wind, and I let go of the kite. Instantly it climbed into the air.

"Let out more line!" I hollered.

"How much?"

"All of it!" I cried.

Stump unspooled, and the yellow owl rose and rose, joining the frenzy high overhead. A second later, the Glove's gray shark soared up to meet it. Next came Tugboat's big pillow of a kite in the shape of a catcher's mitt, followed by the rest of our colorful assortment.

The wind whistled and the kites dipped and bobbed, wings flashing, tails snapping to wake the dead.

We hooted and hollered. Billy Wishes

pumped his fist in excitement. Mr. Bones ran around leaping and licking. I glanced over at Stump and saw that even he, for the first time in days, wore a big smile on his face.

Suddenly the music stopped and a deep voice boomed over the PA system: "And now, the event you've all been waiting for! Highlight of the annual Rambletown Kite Festival: the electrifying, blue-skying, death-defying, high-flying, mind-frying Kite Delight Dogfight!"

Stuff my ears with cotton and lock me in an echo chamber, I'd recognize that buttery voice anywhere: it belonged to none other than Louie "the Lip" Leibenstraub. But the Kite Delight Dogfight? I had no idea what that meant. I must have been the only one, because the crowd let out a deafening whoop.

"If you are not participating in the dogfight," continued the Lip, "now's the time to reel in your kite. I repeat, combatants stay in the air. Everyone else bring down your kites RIGHT NOW."

About half the fliers instantly lowered their kites.

I exchanged glances with Stump.

He shrugged. "Better take her down, I guess," he said, starting to crank.

Before he could make much headway, a menacing red dragon swooped over and smashed my little yellow owl smack between the wings.

"Hey!" Stump shouted. He jerked on the line as the dragon struck again and the crowd roared.

"The battle is drawn!" cried the Lip. "Score one for the dragon!"

As the DJ spoke, the dozen or so kites left in the air launched furious attacks on one another. Jabbing, ripping, pecking, and poking, they tore at one another like enraged hyenas. Wings were shredded, tails torn clean off. One after another, wounded kites crashed to the ground.

"Wait! Wait!" Stump cried, his right arm

jerking wildly on the winder. "I'm trying to get down!"

I reached out to help. "Let me take it," I shouted.

Too late.

The red dragon lunged and dealt another crushing blow.

"No!" Stump shouted, maniacally jerking the string.

"The dragon means business!" cried the Lip. "Can the owl retaliate? Or is this the end for our yellow friend?"

Sensing a kill, three more kites moved in like vultures. One of them, I realized, was Flicker Pringle's Death Star. I glanced around and saw him standing twenty yards to my right, grinning as he played his line. Panicking, Stump yanked on the reel. The owl sliced through its attackers, its wings ensnaring their strings. Stump twitched again. A pair of bats drifted harmlessly away, their lines severed. The Death Star split open and began spiraling out of control.

"Noooo!" Flicker howled as his kite plunged to the ground.

"That's what you get for messing with the best!" Billy Wishes shouted.

"The owl fights back!" roared the Lip. "There's life in it yet."

"Go get 'em, Stump!" Billy cheered, setting off a team chant: "Stump! Stump! Stump!"

More kites joined the fray, swooping, swirling, slamming. It was like a demolition derby, except the punishment was being dished out high in the air. A pirate ship keeled over and plunged, taking down a tattered space shuttle as it fell. Lines frayed, kite frames snapped like toothpicks. A stingray with shredded wings whistled to the ground.

"Oh, the humanity!" wailed the Lip as a blimp crumpled and crashed.

When the action cleared, only four kites still flew: the fierce dragon that had started the mayhem, a mangled blue biplane, a long-tentacled jellyfish—and my owl with Stump at the controls.

On the ground, jacked-up operators took stock of one another. A couple of tall high-school girls, twins by the look of them, owned the wounded biplane. They did not look happy. The other two kites both belonged to adults. A pony-tailed man wearing jeans and a T-shirt controlled the jellyfish, while a slim guy in sunglasses and a red satin windbreaker piloted the fearsome dragon. Gold lettering on the back of his jacket said "Elite Dogfight Club." Underneath that was a motto: "Death from Above." The old guys had both brought their own cheering sections.

"Roll, Jelly, roll!" cheered the fish fans.

The dragon supporters offered nothing so cheerful. Their chant was simple, direct, and chilling:

"Die! Die! Die!"

Smiling wickedly, the assassin in the shiny jacket quickly maneuvered his dragon into the wounded biplane and coolly slashed its line. Instantly the plane spiraled downward, its two crestfallen fliers dashing to intercept it before it broke up on the ground.

"A surgical strike by Fred Smedley," crowed the Lip, as the dragon man turned his sights on Stump. "Can anyone stop the reigning dogfight champ?"

Cap pulled low, Stump desperately paid out line. The owl shot upward at warp speed, smashing into the underside of the hovering jellyfish. Snap! The breaking line sounded like a gunshot. The owl wobbled and broke free, wearing the slack jellyfish like a hat.

"The owl lands a brilliant uppercut," gushed the Lip. "Who saw that coming? But watch out! He's flying blind, and here comes Elite Dogfight's dangerous dragon! Da-dump! Da-dump! Da-dump!"

Stump's arm bounced like a jackhammer. Still the jellyfish clung to his kite, weighing him down. He was dead in the water. Make that

142

the air. Tail flowing, jaws agape, the dragon swooped ever closer. At the controls, the flying ace known as Fred Smedley licked his lips in anticipation.

"Die! Die! Die!" roared the bloodthirsty members of the Elite Dogfight Club as the dragon slashed. "Death from above!"

Mr. Bones ran over and buried his face behind my knees. He couldn't bear to watch. I hardly could, either.

Stump yelped and his chicken wing danced. A spasm ran through the owl. It bounced like a yo-yo on a string.

"Unorthodox!" screamed the Lip. "Unusual! Unconventional! It's the weirdest fighting style I've ever seen!"

Jitterbugging out of control, nowhere to hide, the owl knifed straight into the onrushing dragon. The crowd gasped. It was curtains.

Curtains torn to rags, that is.

I glanced at Fred Smedley. He whipped off his sunglasses and stared, a look of utter shock etched on his face. Way up in the sky, the red dragon stopped slithering. For a second it stood perfectly still. Then it slowly split open right down the middle, its two halves peeling away and falling limply to earth. Stump jiggled his line, and the owl slipped loose from the jelly-fish, whose rainbow tentacles waved good-bye as it fluttered harmlessly away.

"Stump! Stump! Stump!" we roared again.

"A shocking upset," blared the Lip. "Electrifying! Death-defying! High-flying! Mind-frying! Folks, say hello to the new champ!" He stalked over and thrust his microphone in Stump's face.

"What's your name, son?"

"Stump," Stump told him.

"And what's your secret? How'd you do it? How did you take down the Elite Dogfight dragon?"

Stump tugged at his cap. He shrugged. He mumbled something under his breath.

"Speak up," urged the Lip. "The world wants to know."

"The yips," Stump repeated. "The yips did it."

"Folks, give it up for Stump and the Yips, whoever they are!" the DJ urged.

A fresh round of applause rolled over Stump like a wave. Blinking, he acknowledged the crowd with a curt little wave. From where I stood, it was impossible to tell whether he was laughing or crying.

★ CHAPTER 16 ★

Early the next morning, one day to go before the All-Star Game, the team met again at Rambletown Field. In place of bats and gloves, we packed rakes, shovels, hammers, and nails. Gabby showed up too, her camera, as always, at the ready.

Skip Lou met us with a smile. As he had the day before, he carried buckets—two of them this time. We wouldn't be using them for target practice. They were full of green paint.

Mr. Bones gave them a quick sniff, then tore across the outfield and through the opening where the wall had collapsed, making a bee-line straight for the locust trees.

"Stay out of trouble!" I called after him.

"Guys," said Skip Lou, "let's make this place shine!"

He divided us into crews and handed out assignments: one team to raise and paint the wall, another to rake smooth the bare dirt of our once lush field.

Stump, Slingshot, Velcro, the Glove, and I grabbed rakes and got to work breaking up clods of dirt and removing knotted clumps of roots and other bits of vegetation left behind by the grasshoppers. The guys avoided eye contact with Stump. I waited for him to turn his back for a second, then shot a quick glance at Slingshot. He nodded.

Excellent!

The little arts and crafts project at his house had gone off without a hitch the night before. With Stump nearby, we dared not discuss our secret.

Soon a steady chorus of hammer blows provided a rhythmic beat to our work, and we found ourselves in a race with the wall builders to see who would finish first. The guys in the outfield might have won, except we had a secret weapon: Stump. Say what you will about the yips, Stump's flapping elbow served him as well at yard work as it had at kite fighting. He pumped like a piston, driving his rake across the dirt with short, powerful chops.

Following Stump's lead, we made quick work of the dusty job. First the outfield, then the foul territories, finally the infield. Just as we finished, the hammering stopped and a cheer rose from right and center field: the wall was back in place.

Only one question remained: now what?

I mean, what good was a new wall when all it enclosed was a dirt patch? A neatly raked and leveled dirt patch, for sure, but dirt all the same. Fit for beach volleyball maybe, but not baseball. You can't play baseball without a green carpet underfoot. And grass doesn't grow in a day.

My eyes darted to Skip's paint buckets. Surely he didn't mean to paint the field?!

As I contemplated the possibility, a Ramble-town Fire Department tanker, lights flashing, wheeled onto the diamond at the head of a convoy of flatbed trucks. The vehicles swept past us and stopped near second base. A guy wearing an orange safety vest hopped down from the leading flatbed. Like the other trucks, it was piled high with what looked like big tubes of dirt.

"What in the world?" I asked nobody in particular. "Dirt we don't need. Dirt we have in spades."

The driver met Skip in the first-base coach's box, and the two men shook hands. I recognized him as the foreman of the tree-clearing crew Skip had spoken to the day before.

"All set?" he asked. Then, nodding in our direction: "Howdy, fellas."

"I think so," Skip said. "Really appreciate what you're doing, Pepper."

"Not a problem. We're as excited about the game as anyone. About time this town put on an All-Star Game again!"

Skip nodded and the man he called Pepper strode off toward the trucks.

"Holy cow," Stump gushed, his eyes wide. "Is that . . . is it really . . ."

"Yep," said Skip. "My old teammate Pepper McGraw. Pretty good shortstop in his day."

"Only the greatest!" corrected Stump, who knew baseball history like most people know their own names. "No offense, Walloper, but that guy could hit! He once blasted three homers in a single game."

"Actually, it was four." Skip smiled. "And as I recall, he did it more than once."

"He could play defense, too," Gabby said. "My dad tells me stories about some of the catches he made." She took a picture of the legendary ballplayer.

"Still loves Rambletown baseball," Skip said. "He and the boys over at public works have waited a long time for another All-Star Game. They even roped in some buddies at the fire department to make sure it happens. Good bunch of guys."

We watched as a couple of firefighters screwed a hose to a nozzle embedded in the side of their truck. They cranked a valve, and water instantly gushed from the hose. They began spraying the field.

Gabby fired away.

"Should we tell them it's not smoke?" asked Ocho, who had drifted in from the outfield with the rest of the team. "It's only a cloud of dust stirred up by the wind? No fire here. By the way, Walloper, Mr. Bones is totally scoping those grasshoppers. He's parked under the trees like a guard dog."

"Turf," said Skip.

"Turf?" I cried. "You mean that horrible plastic stuff?" I shuddered. I'd almost rather play on a painted field. At least paint wouldn't give you carpet burns when you slid, the way artificial turf did. "Why do they need water for fake grass?"

"Watch."

Starting in left field and working toward right, the firefighters hosed down every inch of Rambletown Field. Pepper McGraw and his gang let the water soak in, then sprang into action. Moving like clockwork, they unloaded the flatbed trucks, dropping big dirt bundles every ten feet or so around the field. Then they unrolled the bundles like rugs, revealing the lushest, thickest, greenest strips of grass—real growing grass—I'd ever seen.

"Turf," repeated Skip, his eyes gleaming. "Honest to goodness, one-hundred-percent natural, field-grown grass. What are you waiting for, guys? Go help lay it. We've got a ball field to get ready and an All-Star Game to play!"

We didn't need to be asked twice.

By lunchtime we had that ball yard looking as good as new. Better, even. The wall stood straight once again and sported a fresh coat of green paint. Springy natural grass blanketed the field, a thousand strips of it fitted seamlessly together like one big jigsaw puzzle.

"Awesome job, guys!" Gabby said. "It looks great." Suddenly she frowned. "In fact, it looks almost too good. It makes me mad that you have to share it with Flicker Pringle and some of those other Haymakers." She spit out the team name like it put a bad taste in her mouth.

"It's the All-Star Game, Gabby," I said. "For one day, we put aside our rivalry."

"I know." She sighed. "I just can't get used to the idea of you and those guys actually playing on the same team."

"Don't worry," I assured her. "Once the game is over and the regular season starts again, we'll still want to beat them."

"You better!" she said.

Before the city crew left, Pepper McGraw shook all our hands and thanked us for helping. When he got to Stump, he drew the shortstop aside and whispered something in his ear.

Stump nodded seriously.

Pepper said something more; then, with a wave, he climbed up into his truck and drove away at the head of a column.

The firefighters stuck around to give the turf a good watering before they, too, called it a day. Two rode in the cab and two more stood on the truck's gleaming silver back bumper.

"See you in the morning, Rounders!" cried

one of the bumper riders as the tanker rolled off the diamond. "We'll be leading the parade!"

The only thing left to do was lay chalk stripes down the lines, and the field would be perfect.

"We'll wait until morning for that," Skip said. "The wind will only carry it away if we do it now."

"What about the locusts?" I asked, warily eyeing the trees just outside the fence. "How do we keep them off the new field for the next twenty-four hours?"

"As long as the wind keeps blowing out toward center, we don't have anything to worry about," Skip answered. "The grasshoppers aren't strong enough to buck the breeze. They can only go where it carries them, and ever since they rode it here in the first place, it's been blowing hard to the east."

I nodded. Made sense. Then I crossed my fingers that the weather wouldn't pitch a changeup.

★ CHAPTER 17 ★

At precisely twenty-eight minutes before nine o'clock that evening, my doorbell rang. The time was critical. Sunset that night occurred at 8:32. I was counting on the dusk to provide cover on our mission.

I was waiting for the chime. Mr. Bones was not. When I opened the door, he blasted through like he was wearing a jet pack.

Slingshot pulled a matador and sidestepped past him into the mudroom.

"Ready?"

"Definitely," I said. "Where's everyone else?"

The pitcher jerked his head in the direction of my front yard. I peered out the door. The whole team plus Gabby stood on the porch. Mr. Bones danced around, leaping and licking, tail wagging a mile a minute. Every last person carried a grocery bag. Slingshot handed one to me, its top rolled tight.

"This is it? It's lighter than I expected."

"They came out beautifully," he said, "ugly as sin. Better get a move on."

I whistled Mr. Bones back into the house. "Sorry, pal," I told him. "It's best if you don't come with us." His ears flopped. His tail drooped. "I'll make it up to you, I promise," I said, patting his head.

Then I called to my mom and dad.

"I'm off."

"No later than nine thirty, Banjie," Mom said from the kitchen. "And, Son?"

"Yes?"

"Good luck."

We set off in a pack, keeping to the wooded side of the street, ready to dive behind a tree or a shrub whenever the headlights of an approaching car pierced the gathering darkness. When the coast cleared, we began moving again. Whipped by the ever-howling wind, treetops cast weird dancing moon shadows across our path.

"I am so sick of this wind," I complained. "It's driving me crazy!"

My teammates murmured in agreement. Everybody had had enough of it.

"It's like some kind of a curse," said Billy Wishes.

"Scientifically speaking, wind is nothing but air pressure," Slingshot said. "Air moving from high pressure to low pressure."

"Say what?" I asked.

"Think of it like a balloon," he explained as we advanced through the night, a secret army. "If you squeeze a balloon, the pressure pushes outward and makes the balloon bulge."

"I get that," I said. "But what squeezes air?"

"Temperature. Cold air is heavier than warm air. The extra weight pulls it down. Warm air, on the other hand, thins out and rises. It weighs less. Scientists call this low pressure."

"I remember learning about this stuff in earth-science class," said Velcro. "As warm air rises, surrounding cool air rushes in to replace it. That's wind."

"Exactly," said Slingshot. "Nothing cursed about it."

"So," said Gabby, "In theory, you could stop wind by balancing the pressure. Like if two fans were aimed directly at each other, they would cancel each other out. No wind."

"I guess what we need is a giant fan," I said.

"In theory," said Slingshot, stopping dead in his tracks. We had reached Stump's street. The Glove and Tugboat peeled off and hid behind a clump of bushes.

"Just pop out for a second when they get close," I reminded them. "Don't give him a good look. Only enough to get him thinking."

The rest of us moved on down the block. At Stump's house, Ocho, Gasser, and Kid Rabbit moved across the lawn and disappeared behind trees. Slingshot peered at the glowing hands of his watch. "Eight forty-five," he announced.

We hurried up the walk and knocked on the door of the large, old house. Stump's mom answered instantly. She had the same red hair as her son, although hers didn't stand straight up.

"Come in, come in," she urged. "They'll be back any minute."

"Hi, Mrs. Plumwhiff," I greeted her. "Where to?"

"I think the basement would be best, don't you, Walloper?" She winked. "I'll send him down to pick up the laundry."

I nodded. Stump's house was more than a hundred years old. It had the creepiest basement I had ever seen. Shadowy, damp, full of cobwebs. When we were little, just going down there used to scare the bejeezus out of us.

Mrs. Plumwhiff showed us down a creaky wooden staircase and into a walled-off laundry area. In a crowd, with the lights on, the place wasn't too awful. Then she withdrew, wishing us luck. A few seconds later, the main lights flicked out and the door at the top of the stairs closed with a thud.

"Positions, everybody," I ordered.

My teammates fanned out against the walls, hiding in whatever nooks and crannies they could find. As soon as they were set, I pulled the cord of a dim overhead light, plunging the basement into total darkness. In the inky murk, plastic bags crinkled as lightly as mice creeping across a floor. I reached into the one I carried and pulled out my mask, slipping it quickly over my head.

Seconds later the door at the top of the stairs creaked open, and the main basement light flared on. Footsteps sounded on the worn wooden treads. Stump was coming down. My heart beat like a drum, pounding so loudly that I feared it would give us away.

When Stump reached the last step, the lights

suddenly went out again.

"Hey!" cried Stump. He hesitated, then I heard him shuffle slowly forward, feeling his way into the laundry room.

Into our trap.

The overhead light snapped on.

"Boo!" we shouted at once, leaping from every corner.

"Aahhh!" hollered Stump. Still gripping the light cord, he sprang backward. The room went dark again. "AAAAGGGHHH!" he yelled even louder than before.

"Stump!" I cried. "Stump! It's us!"

"Turn on the light!" shouted Billy Wishes. "I don't like this!"

Someone found the cord and pulled it. The small room burst into light, revealing Stump sitting on the floor. His stand-up red hair stood taller than ever. It looked like it had tried to leap clean out of the basement.

"You guys scared me out of my wits," Stump panted. "What's the big idea?"

"Sorry, bro," I said, whipping off my papier-mâché mask. "It had to be done." I took his hand and pulled him to his feet. Only then, glancing around at my friends, did I see how gruesome our swampy green grasshopper heads really were, with their clenched jaws, bulging black eyes, and bristling antennae. "You can take them off now, everybody," I said.

One by one, they did.

"Did it work?" Billy asked. "Are you cured?"

"Cured?" Stump asked, still dazed.

"Of the yips," explained Billy. "We figured out that the yips are like hiccups, only they're in your arm instead of where you breathe. And the best way to get rid of hiccups is to get scared real good."

Stump stared at him. His jaw dropped. Then he started to laugh. "The yips are like hiccups," he repeated. "Hey, that's pretty good! Maybe it's all the adrenaline rushing through my body, but I do feel sort of different. Man, you guys surprised me!"

"We figured nothing could be scarier than grasshoppers," chimed in Velcro. "I mean, the trouble started when those things flew down onto the field. That's when you got the yips."

"I knew it," exclaimed Billy. "I knew it would work! You'll play great in the All-Star Game!"

"I'm sure going to try," Stump said.

As we talked, the guys who'd hidden outside bounded down the stairs.

"What'd we miss?" Kid Rabbit panted.

"More of you!" shouted Stump. "You were in the bushes, right? I knew I saw something out there! Freaked me out. My dad told me it was my imagination!"

I was glad Stump was being such a good sport about it.

"Say," I asked him, "what did Pepper McGraw whisper to you this afternoon?"

"Pretty much the same thing you guys have been saying. That the yips are all in my head. He said my aim would come back if I stopped thinking so much about it. That's what finally worked for him."

My eyes widened. "You mean . . ."

"Yep, he once came down with his case of the yips. A bad one. Full body twitches and everything."

Wow. Pretty good company.

Slapping Stump on the back, we climbed the stairs out of the basement. Mr. and Mrs. Plumwhiff waited for us at the top.

"Your friends are good guys, Stump," his mom said. "They planned this whole thing by themselves."

"You call that good?" Stump asked. "They nearly killed me."

But he was smiling. So were his folks.

"Now you kids better run home," his mom said. "Your parents will be waiting. And Stump needs to rest. He has an All-Star Game tomorrow, you know."

We knew, all right.

We said our good-byes and headed back to our own homes.

I didn't know if our trick really had worked. We'd have to wait for the game to find out for sure. But I did know our old pal looked happier than he had in a long time.

★ CHAPTER 18 ★

All night long, the wind screamed like kids on a roller coaster. The windows rattled. The house timbers creaked. The constant noise made it hard to sleep. I tossed like a salad before finally drifting off, worries about the yips and the All-Star Game racing through my head faster even than the air whipped across the night sky.

The relentless gusts must have bothered Mr. Bones, too. Curled up in his usual position at the foot of my bed, he let out a hiccuppy yowl from time to time. His legs churned as he chased something in his dreams. Grasshoppers, most likely.

In the morning I awoke feeling tense. Pulling on my All-Star uniform helped settle my nerves.

Arching white letters on the crisp red jersey announced that I played for the East. The right sleeve bore a blue patch in the shape of a five-pointed star. I'm not ashamed to admit I took a minute to admire myself in the mirror. I felt proud to wear that uniform.

Feeling better, I went downstairs. My dad had beaten me to the kitchen. I found him bunkered behind a tottering wall of pots and pans. Ceramic bowls overflowing with grated cheese, chopped peppers, diced ham, and who knows what else rose from the countertop practically to the ceiling. Enclosed within his fortress, he cracked half a dozen eggs into a stainless-steel mixing bowl and furiously beat them with a wire whisk.

"Today's the day!" he greeted me. "The All-Star Game!"

Seeing him walled off like that reminded

me of the story of Troy and the hollow horse.

"Beware of Greeks bearing gifts," I said.

"Huh?" he asked distractedly. "You want a Greek omelet? We can do that." He poured his goopy mixture onto a sizzling griddle, then clattered the mixing bowl into the sink. "Feta cheese, olives, onions," he mumbled. "I've got them here somewhere."

Dad was like the United Nations of breakfast. He had omelet recipes from every country on earth.

As much as he liked making them, I liked eating them.

Mr. Bones loved them even more.

My dog plopped down next to his dish and swept his tail back and forth across the floor like a broom. The tiles near his feeding station always shined.

I opened the newspaper and turned to the sports section.

A banner headline above a story by Gabby read:

ALL-STARS COME TO TOWN

Led by hometown heroes Ducks Bunion, Stump Plumwhiff, and the Great Walloper, the East All-Stars square off against their counterparts from the West division today at a freshly spruced-up Rambletown Field. Both squads pack ample firepower, stalwart defense, and terrific pitching. With all else being equal, the outcome could hinge on something neither team can control. Namely, the weather.

In a recent game between the Rambletown Rounders and the Hog City Haymakers, the wind whipped like Eddie Shoemaker on the backstretch at Churchill Downs. Fly balls danced like shadow puppets and proved even harder to catch. Routine pop-ups grew wings and soared like eagles. Long fly balls dropped out of the air as suddenly as if they'd run into an invisible wall.

Forecasters predict similar conditions today.

"We expect it to be windier than a politician making a speech," says Rambletown manager Skipper Lou "Skip-to-My-Lou" Clementine.

If he's right, the East may be in trouble. The wacky weather has given fits to starting shortstop Stump Plumwhiff. Against the Haymakers, the normally stellar fielder muffed four straight chances. Any sloppier and you could've slathered his play in tomato sauce, served it up on a hamburger bun, and called it Joe.

Not that you would have found any takers among his steadfast teammates or coach, all of whom refuse to point fingers. "Really difficult conditions," said Skip Lou. "You can't win 'em all."

Not when the wind howls like something out of The Wizard of Oz, you can't. But if Stump doesn't settle down, his team is going to need more than home-field advantage to prevail against the powerful West All-Stars. They'll need a pair of ruby slippers.

I tossed aside the paper. A hard story, but basically fair. Only one part confused me.

"Dad," I asked, "Who is Eddie Shoemaker?"

"He was a professional jockey," Dad said without looking up from the stove. The omelet had reached a delicate stage and required all his attention. "You know, raced horses. Little guy. Rode like the wind."

I let the wind reference pass. Wind wasn't something I wanted to dwell on. "What about Churchill Downs?" I said. "What's that?"

"Famous horse track. Home of the Kentucky Derby, the biggest horse race in the world."

"Do jockeys really whip their horses?" I asked. It sounded cruel.

"I don't know. I guess so." Dad turned the omelet on the griddle, then looked my way. "They carry these springy little sticks called riding crops. Why all the interest?"

"Just an article in the sports pages. I think I get it now."

"About horse racing?"

"About baseball," I said.

"There are no horses in baseball."

"No," I agreed, "but the sport sure can whip you if you're not careful."

Dad shot me a funny look but let it drop. Returning his attention to breakfast, he carefully levered the omelet onto a plate with a pair of spatulas. What he really needed was a crane. Pale yellow and quivery, the thing was the size of the Goodyear blimp.

"Breakfast is served," he said.

"Oh, good," Mom said, coming into the kitchen. "I'm just in time. Morning, guys." Only then did she see the state of the counter. Pots and pans scattered everywhere, bowls spilling ingredients like dirty secrets. She shook her head. She sighed.

Then she started giggling.

"What?" asked Dad, lugging his creation to the table. "Genius at work. Don't worry about it. Your only job is to eat."

"My kind of work," Mom said.

Face flushed, Dad carved the zeppelin into

gargantuan portions and served them up.

"Eat," he said. "There's hits in omelets."

We were about to tuck in when a string of firecrackers exploded in the kitchen. That's what it sounded like. Actually, it was Mr. Bones's stomach grumbling.

"Sorry, pal," I apologized.

I sliced off a hunk of omelet and dropped it into his bowl. The grumbling stopped and the lip smacking began. We followed his example and chowed down.

Eating made me feel better. With each bite, my anxiety about the game lessened. By the time I finished, I was full of more than eggs. I was full of hope about Stump and the yips and the wind and the locusts. It's impossible to worry too much on a full stomach.

"Thanks, Dad," I said. "I needed that."

After breakfast Mom automatically started in on the dishes. Dad pretended to be mad.

"Out," he commanded. "Out of my kitchen. I said I'd clean up and I will."

"My birthday's not until next month." Mom laughed, surrendering the sponge.

I helped Dad scrub. While we worked, Mom entertained us by reading interesting bits from the paper:

"Responding to a noise complaint, police discovered a flock of two hundred Canada geese in the swimming pool of a family on Winterberry Lane. Apparently the birds landed there seeking shelter from the wind.

"While working on a downtown office building, a window washer was picked up by a gust and deposited atop a church steeple three miles away. Frightened but unharmed, he hung by his belt until firefighters rescued him.

"A local couple who went missing three days ago has turned up alive and well at a makeshift campsite in a remote area of

Mitchell County. Rhett and Tara O'Hara
vanished from their farmhouse last Tues-
day. When police found them, Mrs. O'Hara
was frying eggs over an open fire, while her
husband napped in a patio chair. A flock
of chickens scratched nearby. 'One min-
ute I'm hanging out laundry,' Mrs. O'Hara
reported, 'the next here I am plunked down
in the middle of nowhere.' When Mr. O'Hara
awoke, police say he immediately wanted to
know what day it was. 'Have we missed the
All-Star Game?' he asked. The O'Haras agree
that it will be good to get back. 'There's no
place like home,' they said. Authorities con-
tinue to investigate."

With the dishes done, I said good-bye to my
folks and headed off to Rambletown Field on
my bike. I couldn't wait to see how the new turf
had held up through the night.

"See you in the second inning," my parents called from the porch as I pedaled into a

stiff breeze. A very full, very happy Mr. Bones waddled along behind me. The extra weight of the jumbo omelet probably was a good thing. It kept him grounded in all that wind.

★ CHAPTER 19 ★

Rambletown Field buzzed with activity when I arrived. A fire engine flashed in the parking lot. The school marching band warmed up on the infield, trumpets tooting, tubas burping. Baton twirlers pranced in the on-deck area.

The place looked spectacular, not a single blade of grass out of place. Overnight, the wind had remained steady, keeping the grasshoppers pinned in their clump of trees out beyond the outfield wall. Red, white, and blue bunting flapped in the breeze along the grandstand rail. Hundreds of fans already filled the seats, many waving homemade banners hand-lettered with the names of their teams—the Lumleyville

Lumberjacks, the Bixburg Blue Bottles, the Windsor Gaskets, the Pikerton Scrooges, and lots more. One whole cheering section shook cowbells.

Unfortunately, not even the Haymaker rooters drowned out the grasshoppers. They hummed louder than ever. I hoped they weren't getting ready to make a break for it.

I tried to put the bugs out of my mind as I hurried onto the diamond to meet the other All-Stars. The first person I looked for was Stump.

I found him on the top step of the home dugout, surrounded by the rest of the Rounders as he limbered up.

"How are you feeling?" I asked, full of hope.

"Pretty good," he said, flashing a smile. But a certain stiffness in the way he moved told me that all was far from well.

We didn't have time to talk about it before Skip Lou rounded us up for the opening parade. To cries of "Good luck!" from our teammates, Stump, Ducks, and I fell into line with the other

East All-Stars. Mr. Bones came with us. That dog loves parades.

The fire engine rolled onto the field, two firefighters perched on the bumper flinging candy to kids in the stands. The marching band and majorettes massed behind the truck, followed by the players from both teams. Then the truck led us down the first-base line and into right field.

The crowd roared, fans screaming the names of their favorite players: "Mudfish!" "Choo-Choo!" "Slats!" "Flicker!"

We circled the outfield and finished by marching straight down the third baseline. As we neared home, a familiar voice rang out from the crowd.

"Yoo-hoo! Yoo-hoo!"

I looked up and saw the lady from Hog City waving from behind the backstop. Her glittery jewelry sparkled brighter than ever as she stalked on high heels to intercept me at home plate, her pink-bowed Afghan mincing by her side. Leading with his tongue, Mr. Bones rushed to meet them. The woman bent down to pet him and he slapped a wet one on her perfectly made-up face.

"I've been looking for you," the woman sputtered, rising. "Princess Pinky Muffin and I googled "royal Oxford sniffing spaniel" on the internet, and we didn't find a thing, did we, looovy wooovy? Not a thing!"

Uh-oh, I thought.

Suddenly Gasser emerged from the crowd, where he'd been watching.

"Of course you didn't!" he said, elbowing forward. "The breed is way too exclusive for the internet. Plaster the breed all over the Net, suddenly everybody and his brother wants a royal Oxford sniffing spaniel. The association would never stand for it. They prefer to keep ownership by personal invitation only. Keep away the riffraff that way."

"Of course," whispered the woman as I bit my lip to keep from laughing. "The association.

Hush-hush. Invitation only. Well, if you ever decide to breed this adorable creature, please let me know." She slipped me a card. "I can furnish references. Call me."

I waited until she was gone to look at the card. When I did, my jaw nearly hit the ground.

"No way!" I exclaimed.

"What's it say, Walloper?" Ducks demanded.

A yelp of surprise escaped his lips as he read the name spelled out in fancy pink letters on the small rectangle of cardboard:

Mrs. Priscilla Pringle

Sure enough, when I looked up again, I spotted her on the pitcher's mound, posing for a snapshot with her son, the biggest, meanest Haymaker of them all.

Then the umpire cleared the field.

"PLAY BALL!" he barked.

To the roar of the crowd and the grasshoppers, I ran onto the field with the East All-Stars.

Leading off for the West, Grant Vesper of the St. Joe Jungle Cats dug in at the plate.

Flicker Pringle glowered down at him from the hill, rolling his trademark toothpick from side to side in his mouth. For the first time in my life, I didn't mind seeing him do that. He kicked and delivered a sizzling fastball.

Whoosh went the pitch.

"Yowch!" yelled catcher Charlie "Slats" Connolly of the Bixburg Blue Bottles, who wasn't used to Flicker's heat.

"STEE-RIKE ONE!" bleated the ump.

Strike two came hot on its heels, followed by number three. Out in the bleachers, Haymakers fans superglued a red *K* onto our freshly painted wall.

"Way to go, Flicker," I called from third, the words sounding strange even as I spoke them.

I glanced over at press row, where all the reporters sat, and saw Gabby glaring at me. She really had a thing about Flicker.

The big, mean fireballer proceeded to whiff the next two All-Stars in order, both on wicked heaters.

If Flicker kept pitching like that, it wouldn't matter whether Stump's yips had been cured or not. He wouldn't need to make any plays. As it was, our shortstop looked relieved to dash off the field as the top half of the first came to a close.

Hitting for the East in the bottom of the inning, Choo-Choo Choo of the Bixburg Blue Bottles smashed the first pitch he saw up the middle for a base hit. Stump batted next and lashed a single to right. The yips sure didn't affect his hitting any.

Then it was my turn.

As I strode up to the plate, the home crowd stood and cheered. "Give it a ride, Walloper!" someone shouted.

I sure meant to try.

Grant Vesper stared in for a sign. He kicked and delivered. I swung with all my might and hit the ball on the nose. It soared toward center field like it had wings. It might have cleared the wall, too, if only a sudden shift in the breeze hadn't knocked it down. "Lousy low pressure," I muttered, remembering Slingshot's lecture from the night before. The ball bounced on the warning track, and I raced around to third, driving home the first two runs of the game.

When I looked up, I saw Pepper McGraw leaning over the third baseline, clapping like mad. He wore a Rounders cap on his head and a big smile on his face. I was glad he'd seen my triple. I wished my parents had, too. But it was only the first inning, so of course they were killing time in the parking lot.

After my hit, Grant seemed to flip a switch. He started pitching like the All-Star he was and retired the next three batters in a row, ending the inning before we could inflict any more damage.

Neither team managed any base runners in the second. The score held at 2–0. Just as important, the locusts stayed in their trees.

In the third the wind picked up, and the hitting did too. Balls began to fly out of the park.

Cheese Grabini and Chick Hernanski homered for the West. Neither player struck the ball particularly well. Cheese seemed downright surprised to catch a piece of Flicker's fastball. But the wind grabbed both flares and deposited them in the cheap seats. Hoot Fewster answered for us in the bottom half, keeping us ahead by a run, 3–2.

Flicker came out for the fourth on a mission. Still peeved at the freak taters, he blazed one smoking heater after another. Slats yelped a little louder with each pitch as the West went down in order.

The game was more than half over and Stump still hadn't needed to make a throw.

The fifth inning belonged to Ducks. He dived into the left field seats to steal a dinger from Stinkeye Boyle, hitting for the West. Then he clocked one of his own with a runner aboard when it was his turn to bat.

We moved to the sixth and final inning leading 5–2 and feeling pretty good about our chances. For the first time all game, I allowed myself to think we were out of the woods. Neither the yips nor the locusts would mess things up for us.

Shows you how much I know.

CHAPTER 20

"**B**ATTER UP!" cried the ump.

Flicker blazed two darts past the West leadoff man, Snapper Po. Then he scorched another. But poor Slats, his hand tenderized by the constant pounding, couldn't hold onto it. The ball squirted away from our catcher, and Snapper alertly scampered to first on a dropped third strike.

The next guy up tried to bunt, always risky against Flicker. Shocking us all, he managed to push the ball past the pitcher without splintering his bat. Stump raced in and made a bare-handed grab at the edge of the infield grass. I held my breath as he turned toward second to start a double play. It was his first chance of the game. And I let it out in a groan when his toss sailed wide, pulling second baseman Bunker Dodge off the bag. Both runners were safe.

Flicker took the ball back and glowered first at Slats, then at Stump.

"You clowns call yourselves All-Stars?" he growled. "My dog plays better defense."

He proceeded to drill the very next batter square in the hip to load the bases. Behind the plate, Slats Connolly looked relieved that he didn't have to catch the ball for once.

"TAKE YOUR BASE!" commanded the ump, staring daggers at Flicker as the pitcher rolled his toothpick around in his mouth.

I don't know if Flicker hit the batter on purpose. Maybe it was his warped way of sending a message after two guys reached base on errors. I wouldn't put it past him. If so, he didn't accomplish anything except to bring the go-ahead run to the plate with no outs. Fortunately

Flicker fanned the next guy on three invisible hummers. A real fan would have been nice. We could have used it to balance the treacherous wind.

As it was, the gale grew more powerful by the second. It ripped through the park like it had claws, tearing the bunting off the grand-stand and shredding the collection of red *K*s that Flicker's fans had posted on the outfield wall. In the bleachers spectators clung to one another for dear life. One false move and they'd be swept away forever.

Given the conditions, Stump didn't stand a chance when the next batter slashed a grounder toward the hole. Ranging to his right, the short-stop backhanded it neatly and came up gunning for the lead runner.

As Stump fired home, a gust rocked the grandstand. The locusts screamed. Mr. Bones raced to the top of the dugout steps and barked a blue streak. Stump's elbow danced a jig—and his toss sailed over the runner, over the catcher, over the umpire, over everything.

One base runner crossed the plate standing. A second followed hot on his heels. All of a sudden, our lead was down to a single run.

Forgetting themselves in the excitement, West fans jumped out of their seats to cheer. Those who leaped too high instantly were carried off on the jet stream.

"Time out!" I called.

I trotted over to Stump.

"Feel like catching a movie after the game?" I asked.

He looked at me like I had two heads.

"I hear *Sherlock Drones: Detective Wars* is pretty good." I'd read somewhere that when pro ballplayers huddled, the smart ones talked about anything other than the game. The idea was to break the tension.

My ploy didn't work on Stump. He ground his toe into the dirt, mute as a stone.

"Okay, forget it," I said. "Just keep cool. Pepper McGraw told you to chill, right? You should listen to him. It's all in your head."

I was about to say more when Flicker Pringle elbowed me out of the way.

"Listen, chump," he growled, jabbing Stump in the chest. "You blow one more easy out, you're toast."

I gaped. Nothing like supporting a teammate.

Stump's eyes flashed. His nostrils flared. He squared his shoulders and found his voice. "Just pitch the ball, Princess Pinky Muffin."

The fearsome pitcher nearly choked on his toothpick. Jaw clenched, he stomped back up the mound without another word. Way to go, Stump!

We slapped mitts and I jogged into position.

"PLAY BALL!" cried the ump as heavy-hitting Gravedigger Veach dug in at the plate and base runners danced at second and third.

Flicker kicked and delivered.

First-pitch swinging, Gravedigger lashed a line drive over my head. The ball rocketed halfway to the left-field foul pole, then changed its mind and turned hard to the right. Borne by the wind, it crossed the entire width of the out-field before Buttered Toast tracked it down in the farthest reaches of right field for out number two. The base runners trotted back to their bags.

Spared disaster by the wind and a heads-up play by our right fielder, Flicker Pringle went back to work. He hurled two strikes past Mud-fish LaRouche of the Pikerton Scrooges. One more would end the game. A hit would give the West the lead because with two outs, the runners would surely sprint on contact and the guy on second wouldn't stop until he slid home with the go-ahead run. The drama pulled fans to the edge of their seats. East fans cheered themselves hoarse. Those rooting for the West simply prayed.

Flicker delivered. Mudfish checked his swing.

"BALL ONE!" declared the ump.

A second ball followed, just off the inside corner.

Half the crowd groaned. The other half sighed with relief.

Out in the trees, every last grasshopper shrieked.

I glanced over at Stump. He stared home with steely concentration.

Mudfish fouled off the next pitch. Then he fouled off two more, keeping the West's hopes alive. A frustrated Flicker missed outside to fill the count: three balls, two strikes.

I glanced around the diamond. The base runners were coiled like Olympic sprinters waiting for the starting gun. With two outs and the game on the line, they surely would take off for home on Flicker's next pitch. I dropped into a crouch, ready to spring at the ball if it came my way.

"Let's go, East," I called. "Let's win this thing!"

Flicker brought his hands together above

his head. Mudfish cocked his bat. The runner on second inched toward third. The runner on third leaned for home. The wind hammered. The locusts wailed.

Just then, a yellow comet streaked across the grass.

"Mr. Bones!" I shouted after it. "Come back!"

He did not come back. He flashed through the outfield and leaped the wall at a single bound.

By then the pitch was halfway to the plate. Mudfish met it with a wicked swing. Right up the middle the ball bounded.

Right at Stump.

The shortstop speared the blast on one bounce and turned toward first, where big Hoot Fewster opened his glove to receive the throw. As Stump gripped the ball, a mighty *whoosh* filled the air. Out of the corner of my eye, I saw Slats fling off his mask and point toward the sky.

"Oh, Mr. Bones!" I cried. For I knew right

then that my dog had finally rousted his mortal foes. The grasshoppers rose from the trees in a great, darkening cloud.

For a split second longer, the wind gusted as if it aimed to blow Rambletown Field clean off the map.

Then, abruptly, it stopped, checked at last by the combined power of ten billion pairs of wings beating hard against it.

Air pressure! I thought.

Stump never wavered. In the sudden calm, he whipped the ball. The red-stitched orb spun through the still air and found its mark, straight and true.

"OUT!" bayed the ump as the ball settled into Hoot's outstretched mitt.

His cry seemed to break a spell.

Arms raised high, Hoot leaped into the air. Stump ran to meet him. I raced to join the party. Everybody else had the same idea at the same time, including Mr. Bones, who careened across the field and pounced on Stump's back,

195

riding him to the ground. Before I knew exactly what happened, I found myself rolling in a giant pig pile on the sweet, soft grass.

"Nice throw, buddy!" I shouted.

"Nothing to it," came Stump's muffled reply from somewhere below me.

Then I turned over on my back and looked up at the sky.

Not a locust in sight. As surely as Stump's yips, they had vanished.

I hoped never to see either again.

RAMBLETOWN ROUNDERS LINEUP

PLAYER	POSITION	THROWS	BATS
Ducks Bunion	left field	left	left
Stump Plumwhiff	shortstop	right	right
The Great Walloper, Banjo H. Bishbash	third base	right	right
Orlando "Velcro" Ramirez	center field	left	left
Tugboat Tooley	catcher	right	right
Gilly Wishes	first base	left	left
Slingshot Slocum	pitcher	right	right
Octavio "Ocho" James	right field	right	right
Ellis "the Glove" Rodriguez	second base	right	right
Gasser Phipps	center field	right	right
Kid Rabbit Winkle	substitute third base	right	right
Skipper Lou "Skip-to-My-Lou" Clementine	manager		

EAST ALL-STARS

PLAYER	POSITION	TEAM
Flicker Pringle	pitcher	Hog City Haymakers
Charlie "Slats" Connolly	catcher	Bixburg Blue Bottles
Hoot Fewster	first base	Hog City Haymakers
Bunker Dodge	second base	Lumleyville Lumberjacks
The Great Walloper, Banjo H. Bishbash	third base	Rambletown Rounders
Stump Plumwhiff	shortstop	Rambletown Rounders
Ducks Bunion	left field	Rambletown Rounders
Choo-Choo Choo, the "Steam Engine"	center field	Bixburg Blue Bottles
Medric "Buttered Toast" Salazar	right field	Camden Clockers

WEST ALL-STARS

PLAYER	POSITION	TEAM
Grant Vesper	pitcher	St. Joe Jungle Cats
Mudfish LaRouche	catcher	Pikerton Scrooges
Cheese Grabini	first base	Sand Hill Rooks
Cesar "Hot Pocket" Escalante	second base	Attitash Rowdies
Cannonball Crawford	third base	Windsor Gaskets
Snapper Po	shortstop	Pikerton Scrooges
Linus "Stinkeye" Boyle	left field	Windsor Gaskets
Chick Hernanski	center field	St. Joe Jungle Cats
Eddie "Gravedigger" Veach	right field	Laconia Poets

MORE RAMBLETOWN ROUNDERS STATS

PLAYER	HEIGHT	WEIGHT	LITTLE-KNOWN FACT
Ducks Bunion	4' 4"	75	Ducks holds the neighborhood pogo stick record—1037.
Stump Plumwhiff	4' 1"	64	Stump owns a complete set of Major League baseball cards for every year since he was born.
The Great Walloper, Banjo H. Bishbash	4' 5"	73	Walloper loves to read mystery stories, particularly the Phantom Association books.
Orlando "Velcro" Ramirez	4' 4"	74	For Halloween, Orlando dressed up as the masked swordsman Zorro.
Tugboat Tooley	4' 9"	85	Tugboat's favorite insect is the Madagascar hissing cockroach.
Gilly Wishes	4' 6"	80	Gilly once laughed so hard he passed part of a hot dog through his nose.

PLAYER	HEIGHT	WEIGHT	LITTLE-KNOWN FACT
Slingshot Slocum	4' 5"	72	Slingshot built a model volcano for the fourth-grade science fair. It blasted the school ceiling with a stream of foamy red liquid.
Octavio "Ocho" James	4' 4"	74	When Octavio was home-schooled, he learned to count to twenty in six different languages, including Mandarin Chinese.
Ellis "the Glove" Rodriguez	4' 3"	69	With his lightning reflexes, Ellis caught a fly with his bare hand — the insect kind of fly, not the baseball kind.
Gasser Phipps	4' 8"	84	Gasser can recite the entire alphabet while burping.
Kid Rabbit Winkle	4' 2"	67	After baseball, Kid Rabbit's second-favorite sport is track and field, especially the long jump.

GRAND SLAM

R

R

Alex Plumwhiff
"Stump"
Rambletown Rounders

Shortstop

EXTRAS

The Super Sluggers
WING DING

**Kevin Markey's Ten Truly Wacky Moments
in Baseball History**

Weirdest Baseball Jargon

Kevin Markey's Top Five Baseball Movies to "Catch"

**An Exclusive Sneak Peek at the next book
in the Super Sluggers series, *Rainmaker***

Kevin Markey's Ten Truly Wacky Moments in Baseball History

Run, Red, Run!

On July 14, 1915, Chicago White Sox pitcher Red Faber reached first during a game against Philadelphia. With rain on the way, Faber came up with a crazy way to speed along the inning: he tried to get picked off the base on purpose! When the opposing pitcher ignored Faber's huge lead, he reluctantly stole second. Once more he wandered off the bag and, again, the defense paid no attention to him. So Faber waltzed down to third. By then he must have figured that the quickest way to get off the field would be to steal home. So he did. And the rain never came!

Babe and the Pup

One time in 1923 when the Yankees were beating the White Sox in Chicago, a puppy somehow got loose from the stands and started running around left field. The Babe got down on all fours to play with the dog, who grabbed Ruth's glove and trotted away—while the Yankee pitcher kept throwing. Sure enough, the Chicago batter lifted a high fly ball—right toward Ruth! The Bambino jumped up and caught the ball bare-handed. Then he raced after the puppy to get his glove back.

Did He or Didn't He?

During the 1925 World Series between the defending champion Washington Senators and the Pittsburgh Pirates, fans who sat in the extra seats in the outfield of Washington's Griffith Stadium got a close-up view of one of the wackiest plays in World Series history.

In the eighth inning of the third game, the Pirates' Earl Smith smashed a deep drive. Right fielder Sam Rice went back, way back . . . and crashed head-over-heels into the temporary bleachers. Swallowed by the crowd, Rice and the ball disappeared from view. As the umpire raced over to see what was going on, the right fielder suddenly popped onto the field with the ball planted firmly in his glove. "Out!" cried the ump. Pittsburgh protested, but the call stood and Washington won the game. Many years later Rice gave a sealed envelope to the Baseball Hall of Fame and asked that it be opened after he died. It turned out to hold a letter in which he wrote, "At no time did I lose possession of the ball."

World's Smallest Strike Zone

During a 1951 game against the Detroit Tigers, a little person named Eddie Gaedel, wearing a complete St. Louis Browns uniform with the number 1/8 on the back, strolled up to the plate to bat lead-off for the Browns. Standing 3' 7" in his spikes, the guy was about a foot shorter than the average Little Leaguer. His strike zone was only an inch and a half high! Detroit protested, but it was all perfectly legal. Browns owner Bill Veeck had actually signed Gaedel to a one-game contract!

Never Mind

The New York Mets joined the National League in 1962 and had one of the worst seasons ever. One player who stood out was first baseman Marvin Eugene Throneberry, and not just because his initials spelled MET. Among Marvelous Marv's legendary blunders was a base-running mistake in a game against the Cubs on June 17. Batting in the bottom of the first, he cracked a deep drive and raced all the way around to third with a triple. Unfortunately, Throneberry ran right over first base without ever touching it and the ump called him out. Mets manager Casey Stengel charged out of the dugout to protest. "Don't bother, Casey," the ump told him. "He missed second too!"

That's Using Your Head

Aging slugger and noted goofball José Canseco was playing right field for the Texas Rangers in a game against Cleveland on May 26, 1993. Carlos Martinez came to the plate for the Indians and launched a long fly ball. Canseco gave chase but somehow lost sight of the ball as it plummeted from the sky near the warning track. The ball landed squarely on his head . . . and bounced over the wall for a home run! A professional indoor soccer team saw the clip and offered Canseco a contract.

Hitless Wonder

Rockies catcher Ben Petrick set a Major League record on September 20, 2000, by collecting four RBI—without getting a single hit! Petrick knocked in a run on a groundout in the second inning, had a sacrifice fly in the fourth, drove in a run on another groundout in the eighth, and drew a bases-loaded walk in the ninth for his fourth and final RBI of the game.

Nine-in-One

Against the White Sox on September 6, 2000, Scott Sheldon entered the game in the fourth inning as a substitute catcher. He moved to first base in the fifth inning, before going over to second base and then shortstop in the sixth. By the time the game ended, Sheldon had played all nine positions—including pitcher, where he struck out the only batter he faced on a 67-mile-per-hour changeup!

Home Run! You're Out!

With teammate Miguel Tejada on first base in an April 2006 game against the Angels, Javy Lopez of Baltimore smashed a deep drive. As center fielder Darin Erstad gave chase, Tejada started motoring around the bases. Erstad leaped at the wall, then tumbled to the ground. Thinking the center fielder had made a spectacular catch, Tejada retreated back toward first base. Running hard all the way, Lopez went right past him. That's when Erstad got up off the ground, dusted himself off, and held up his empty glove: Lopez's hit had cleared the wall for a homer. The ump waved Tejada home, but Lopez was called out for passing the runner in front of him, a definite no-no in baseball.

A Plague of Gnats

On October 5, 2007, Yankee reliever Joba Chamberlain stood on the mound at Cleveland's Progressive Field in game two of the American League division series. It was the bottom of the eighth, Yankees leading 1–0. New York was six outs away from winning the game and evening the series. Suddenly a massive cloud of tiny black biting insects invaded the infield. The bugs swarmed Chamberlain, getting in his eyes, nose, ears, and mouth. Flailing like a windmill, he walked a batter. Then he threw a wild pitch. The bugs kept biting and Chamberlain fired another wild pitch, allowing the tying run to score. Soon afterward a breeze blew up and the insects vanished, but the damage had been done. The Indians went on to win the game in eleven innings.

Weirdest Baseball Jargon

Part of the fun of baseball is the unique language. Here are a few of my favorite words and phrases.

Baltimore chop—A hit that bounces almost straight down in front of home plate and soars over the infield. Back in the early days of baseball, pro players used to intentionally smack choppers by swinging down on the ball. The Orioles groundskeeper was known for packing down the dirt around the plate until it was rock hard, making Baltimore the home of the chop.

Bronx cheer—Boos from the crowd. In other words, the exact opposite of a cheer. The Bronx is home to the Yankees, whose fans have been known to razz visiting players—especially if they come from Boston! Originally a Bronx cheer meant the farting sound a person can make by sticking out his tongue and blowing. Now it refers to lusty hooting in general.

Can of corn—An easy catch by a fielder (the ball falls heavily into his glove like a can of corn).

Cheese—A blazing fastball, preferably one up around the batter's chest—in which case it's called "high cheese." The term possibly comes from old-fashioned British slang for something really good, as in "Blimey, mate, the queen's new horse carriage is the cheese."

Chin Music—A high and inside pitch that roars in under the batter's chin. Definitely not the kind of music a hitter likes to hear.

Gopher ball—A home run, as in the outfielder has to "go for" the ball a long, long way without success.

Moon Shot—A sky-high home run.

Hit the ball on the screws—To really rip it; two other ways to hit the ball are "on the button" and "on the nose."

Rabbit Ears—Sensitivity to jeering from the fans. A thin-skinned player is said to have "rabbit ears" because he hears everything (especially Bronx cheers).

Rain bringer—A ball hit so high that it disappears into the clouds.

Seeing-eye single—A soft ground ball that manages to roll into the outfield for a hit, eluding infielders (as if it has eyes).

Texas Leaguer—A bloop hit that lands between the infielders and the outfielders. According to baseball legend, a player named Ollie Pickering rattled off seven straight bloopers while playing for the old Texas League in the 1890s. Announcers soon started calling any ball struck weakly over the infield a Texas Leaguer.

Uncle Charlie—A curve ball. The origins of this term are murky, but many believe it comes from the spelling alphabet used by pilots, in which every letter is assigned a code word: A = Alpha, B = Bravo, etc., all the way to Z = Zulu. "Charlie" is code for C, the first letter in curve.

Kevin Markey's Top Five Baseball Movies to "Catch"

The Pride of the Yankees (1942)
Classic true story of Lou Gehrig, the great Yankee first base-man and teammate of Babe Ruth, who played almost fourteen full seasons without missing one single game. Struck down in his prime by a rare disease, Gehrig stirringly told the 60,000 fans who turned out to see his last game, "Today, I consider myself the luckiest man on the face of the earth."

Angels in the Outfield (1951)
Late one night at the ballpark, bad-tempered Pittsburgh Pirates manager Guffy McGovern runs into the archangel Gabriel. Gabriel has a deal to offer: if the Pirates quit their constant cursing and fighting, the angels will help them climb out of their usual place in the cellar. Miracle follows upon miracle in this fantastically fun tall tale.

The Bad News Bears (1976)
The Bears are possibly the worst Little League team of all time. Spurred to action, their coach, gruff ex-minor leaguer Morris Buttermaker, brings in a couple of unlikely saviors: Amanda, a tomboy pitcher with electric stuff, and Kelly, a wisecracking juvenile delinquent who is the best ballplayer anyone has ever seen. The underdog Bears go on a tear that takes them all the way to a championship showdown against their bratty arch-rivals, the Yankees.

Tiger Town (1983)
Alex's favorite team is the Tigers and his favorite player is

aging star Billy Young, who dreams of making it to the World Series. One day Alex closes his eyes and wishes for Billy to hit a homer. Lo and behold, it happens! Convinced that he controls the Tigers' destiny, Alex starts willing them to victory. The only catch is that he has to be at the game for his super-fan powers to work, and bullies have stolen his ticket to the decisive final game.

Rookie of the Year (1993)

Baseball-crazy twelve-year-old Henry Rowengartner breaks his arm diving for a fly ball. When the cast comes off, he and a couple friends celebrate by going to a Cubs game at Wrigley Field. Henry catches a homerun hit by an opposing player and, in best Chicago tradition, tosses the ball back onto the field. Miraculously, he guns a perfect strike to the catcher standing at home plate, more than 400 feet away! His broken arm has healed with super strength. The Cubs recruit Henry on the spot and he pitches them to the World Series.

Pitching in a light drizzle for the Rambletown Ramblers, Slingshot Slocum kicked high and fired his twelfth pitch of the inning.

The Lumleyville Lumberjack hitter grinned as the ball sailed wide, slapping into Tugboat Tooley's big pie plate of a catcher's mitt a good foot outside the strike zone. It might as well have missed by a mile.

"BALL FOUR!" barked the umpire. "TAKE YOUR BASE!"

The batter didn't need an invitation. He was already trotting up the line, the third straight Lumleyville hitter to draw a walk.

Normally Slingshot is lights out. Now he had loaded the bases in a playoff game. With nobody out, and leading by only a run, we were in a jam.

Against the lowly Lumberjacks, no less.

Don't get me wrong. I have nothing against the Lumberjacks. They're a good bunch of guys. Friendly, cheerful, never spit on their palms for the postgame hand slap. They just happen to stink at baseball.

Year after year, Lumleyville fields one of the worst teams in the ten-to-twelve division. Put it this way: The Lumberjacks are much better at chopping lumber than at swinging it. It was shocking that they had even made the playoffs. Meanwhile, we're pretty good. Usually.

After all, we're the defending champs.

At the moment, we looked more like chumps than champs. Another walk and the Lumberjacks would tie the score. A hit would blow the game wide open. A loss would end our season.

The thought of bowing out in the first round of the playoffs was horrible. From opening day, way back in Rambletown's freakishly frigid spring, our team goal had been to make it to the title game. We had worked our tails off all summer, knowing we would never get another chance to play for the championship. This was our last year together as a team. Next season, a bunch of us would be moving up to a new age bracket. None of us knew which of a dozen different teams we might wind up on. Only one thing was certain:

Soon the Rambletown Rounders as we loved them would be finished. More than anything, we wanted to go out with a bang. We wanted to win one last title.

If we somehow survived the playoffs, we fully expected to face the Hog City Haymakers in the championship game. When it came to winning pennants, our archrivals were like the Pizza Palace of baseball. They delivered. The Haymakers have a pitcher named Flicker Pringle who leads the league in wins, strikeouts, and earned run average. Not to mention brushback pitches, high cheese, and chin music. In other words, he's not afraid to go after batters. Flicker believes home plate belongs to him alone. The rest of us approach it at our own peril.

On top of being scary good, Flicker Pringle and the Haymakers are big. Big and mean and hairy. Half the guys on that team have beards. Pretty strange for a bunch of eleven-year-olds. The other half look like they spend their free time messing around with pianos. Lifting them, not playing them.

As surely as the distance from home to first is sixty feet, the road to the pennant ran through the Haymakers. But first we had to take care of the Lumberjacks.

"Settle down now, kid!" I called from my position at third base as Tugboat gunned the ball back to Slingshot.

Our pitcher snapped the ball out of the mist with a look of disgust. He mopped his face with his sleeve. He stared home for the sign. Tugboat flashed one finger: fastball. Slingshot shook him off. Tugboat gave him the sign for changeup. Slingshot shook him off again.

I groaned. I hoped Slingshot wasn't thinking about throwing the forkball. For some reason known only to himself, lately Slingshot had been obsessed with mastering the forkball, a kind of pitch that dives away from batters before reaching the plate. It's called a forkball because of the grip: You spread your index and middle fingers wide and fork the ball between them. The problem is, the forkball is a terrible pitch if you're a kid. You have to snap your wrist hard to make the

14

ball spin, and the strain can really mess up your arm. No one younger than seventeen or eighteen should fool with it. Everybody knows that. And yet Slingshot kept trying.

The other problem with the forkball was accuracy. Slingshot's version of it was like a bacon double cheeseburger at a vegetarian restaurant. It never crossed the plate.

"Nothing fancy!" I called. "Just hum it in there!"

Slingshot brought his hands together over his head.

That's when the rain really began to fall.

Only "fall" is not the right word for what the rain did. It crashed upon Rambletown Field like a tidal wave, a sudden, drenching wall of water. And it kept right on pounding.

Mayhem erupted in the bleachers as fans scrambled to escape the deluge. As wet as it was, they could've used scuba gear. We could have, too. Or maybe a submarine. Within seconds, the field flooded. So much water fell so fast that the bases rose and began drifting around the swamped diamond, Lumleyville runners clinging to them like Titanic survivors.

"The runners are going!" I shouted as water swirled up to my ankles. Between the hammering rain and all the thunder, no one heard me.

Fortunately, it didn't matter. As I shouted, the umpire jumped from behind the plate. He raised his arms and called off the game.

At least I think he did. It was hard to tell. The solid rush of water from the sky blurred everything like a shower curtain. For all I know, the ump might have been casting a net into the rolling sea.

In any case, I didn't wait for a second opinion. I waded off the field and into the shelter of the dugout, where Mr. Bones greeted me with a wet smack on the chops.